the
unrepentant
siren

Karen M. Bence

Karen M Bence

SterlingHouse Publisher, Inc. **PITTSBURGH, PA**

8th Crow Books

ISBN-10: 1-56315-438-2
ISBN-13: 978-1-56315-438-6
Trade Paperback
© Copyright 2011 Karen M. Bence
All Rights Reserved
Library of Congress #2011927061

Requests for information should be addressed to:
SterlingHouse Publisher, Inc.
3468 Babcock Blvd.
Pittsburgh, PA 15237
info@sterlinghousepublisher.com
www.sterlinghousepublisher.com

8th Crow Books
is an imprint of SterlingHouse Publisher, Inc.

Cover Design: Nicole Tibbitt
Interior Design: Nicole Tibbitt

Printed in U.S.A.

ACKNOWLEDGEMENTS

I would like to thank a number of people who have supported the development of *The Dark Whispers Series* and, more specifically, this novel. Cindy Sterling of SterlingHouse Publisher, Inc. took a chance on a fledgling author, encouraging me to explore the possibility of developing a series out of *Midnight Revelations*. Megan Davidson, my editor, who makes me look brilliant. My agent, Valerie Clark, has been a mentor, advocate and friend. Suzanne Nash of *Bookworm Reviews* and *Scribe House* bit her lip and agreed to read a book written by a friend of friend, an action that can surely dent any relationship. As a result, *Midnight Revelations – vol.1 in The Dark Whispers Series* was launched with a brilliant review in hand and I gained a good friend. Dorene Briggs has provided lasting friendship filled with many colorful and inspiring adventures. As I wrapped up the final chapters of *The Unrepentant Siren*, I was invited to be a guest at *The Page Turner's Guild*. I found the feedback so insightful I asked them to read and comment on the first draft of *The Siren*. Thankfully, four members agreed: Karen Williamson, Rosanna Beebe, Carolyn Atchison Wailes, and Barbara Davis. I think their suggestions helped to shape a better story. Lisa Keller, who offered to read and make suggestions on improving the rough draft. And to my fans, I hear you…I'm writing as fast as I can. Thank you for picking my books up and giving them a chance. I would be terribly remiss if I didn't say that I am eternally grateful for the unwavering support offered by my wonderful family and fiercely loyal friends. My husband, Bob, is one of those characters that readers find "unbelievable" in *fiction,* but surprisingly pop up every once in a while in the *real world*. I am so blessed he lives in mine.

This book is dedicated to the girls who
rode at Unicorn Farms... and Glenn.

CHAPTER ONE

Hooves pounded out a steady rhythm on the thick Virginia turf. Sara brought her shoulders up and back, opening up the angle of her hip. At the same time, she closed her fingers on the rubberized reins, asking her mount to shift his center of gravity back to his hind end. The final jump was four strides off. Sara instinctively counted down each beat, and then in one fluid movement her arms and torso followed the crest of Gale Force's athletic body as he soared over the stone wall. The horse's front legs curled for a second then straightened out to meet the ground, landing with perfect precision.

Sara stroked the animal's sweaty gray neck with her gloved hand as she eased him down to a trot. "Good boy," she said.

Emma, Sara's English groom, was sitting on another horse at the edge of the course. "Well done," she called to her boss.

Sara smiled and headed in that direction. "Practically flawless," she said, catching her breath. "He's going to kick butt at the horse trial next weekend."

Emma laughed. "Doesn't he always?"

Sara nodded in agreement. They rarely placed outside of the top three in any competition.

The two riders slipped the horses the reins, letting them stretch their tired muscles as they leisurely walked toward the barn.

In the driveway, a sleek, black BMW sport coupe was slicing a wide swath through freshly fallen leaves, creating a fluttering wave in its wake. When it rolled to a stop near the house, Leila, Sara's oldest and best friend, climbed out.

"Why is she here on a Monday morning?" Emma asked as she swatted away a hovering fly.

"Not a clue," Sara answered. She thought about Leila's chosen profession as an interior designer. "Maybe she has a client out this way."

Leila spotted them and waved both arms over her head. She was yelling, but it was too far away for anything to be understandable. Sara and Emma waved back, but didn't hasten their relaxed pace.

"Is she still dating that bloke with the vineyard?" Emma asked.

"Sure is," Sara answered, with a sideways glance. "She may have stayed there last night and decided to swing by here on her way back to Leesburg. Check that out." Sara pointed at Leila and laughed as she watched what could only be described as an uncoordinated game of hopscotch. "What the heck is she doing?"

"She's probably wearing a pair of ridiculously expensive designer heels and is trying like mad to avoid the puddles left over from last night's rain," Emma replied.

Sara pictured Leila's drenched feet and cringed. Whatever her friend was here to say must be pretty darn important for her to risk destroying her shoes as well as her mood. *I bet you're cursing up a wicked storm of your own right now*, she thought.

Sara and Emma were a little less than two hundred yards away when Leila scrambled over to a golf cart parked near the side entrance to the stable.

An electric chill ran up Sara's spine. "Is that still charging?" she asked as she saw Leila reach for the metal bar that supported the cart's little green roof.

"It should be," Emma answered. "Why?"

An agonized whine drifted across the fields on the autumn breeze. The sound startled the horses, causing them to lift their heads and snort nervously.

Sara watched in horror as Leila's body moved in sudden

spastic jerks. Her friend's knees buckled, sending her body crumbling to the soaked ground. In spite of gravity pulling on Leila's weight, the limp woman's hand stayed stubbornly glued to the electrified cart.

"Holy crap," Sara screamed, kicking Gale Force into a gallop.

Emma sprinted up beside her panicked employer. "It must have lost its ground," she yelled over the sound of thunderous hooves.

They arrived back at the barn to find Leila's unconscious body dangling awkwardly from the golf cart as rhythmic spasms jolted her about like a worn rag doll. Smoke wafted off her singed hair like some cartoonish special effect. The farm's dogs, which were previously lounging inside, darted back and forth, barking incessantly at her convulsing limbs.

"Oh, no!" Sara cried, launching herself out of her saddle.

"Don't touch her!" Emma warned, already on the ground and running to the door. "You'll end up the same way. We have to sever the connection to the power."

Sara frantically looked around for something that could be used to break the connection but didn't see anything. "Hurry, she's dying."

"We're good!" Emma yelled, her voice vibrating with urgency. "The master switch is off." When she reappeared, she was carrying an empty plastic feed bucket. She immediately hurled it toward Leila's arm, knocking it free from the metal frame.

Leila's shoulders and head slid down to the gravel drive. It took a minute for her twitching muscles to relax. The seizure passed, but then her eyes rolled back. The dogs paced nervously, all the while crying and moaning. Even they knew the situation was taking a turn for the worse.

"Oh, shit! Leila! Can you hear me?" Sara asked, reaching

out with two fingers to feel for a pulse on the side of her motionless friend's neck. Nothing.

Emma dropped to Sara's side and asked, "Is she breathing?"

"I don't think so," she said. "Call 911. Quick!"

Emma unclipped her phone from a holder attached to her belt. "Bollocks, my cell is out of power. Do you have yours?"

Sara shook her head. "I accidentally left it in the house this morning."

"Tremendous! I'll be right back." Emma got up and ran inside the barn.

In the meantime, Sara checked again for a pulse and leaned in close to Leila's face to feel for even the slightest hint of a breath. "Damn it, Leila. Don't do this to me!"

She cocked Leila's head back, blew two full breaths into her relaxed lungs, then started rapid chest compressions. After 30 thrusts came two more breaths. Sara rechecked the vein along Leila's neck. No response.

"Come on. Don't give up that easily. Fight!" Sara pleaded as she resumed her efforts.

"The ambulance is on its way," Emma said, returning from the office. "The operator said to start CPR if necessary."

"28, 29, 30…got that covered," Sara answered.

Emma squatted down on the opposite side of Leila's laid out body. "Oh bloody 'ell. Look at this," she said, lifting up the unconscious woman's left arm. "The palm of her hand and all her fingers had turned a sickening shade of red and the skin was already blistered.

Sara cringed. "Oh, that's bad. This can't be happening."

Then Emma turned the burned hand around and Sara froze mid-compression. Wrapped around Leila's finger was a huge diamond engagement ring.

"Now I'm really going to be sick," Sara said, looking

down at Leila's unresponsive body underneath her hands. Sara made a fist and pounded on her friend's chest as tears spilled out of her eyes. "Leila, get back in your damn body! You're not getting away with this. You hear me? You are not going to die on me. We have a wedding to plan. Don't throw away this chance at happiness. If not for yourself, do it for Alex. Don't give up now. Leila, please, come back!"

Sara forced air into Leila's mouth, blowing hard enough to reach her friend's deflated lungs. This time, Leila's body jolted back to life. She choked and coughed, gasping painfully for air. After a moment or two, her eyes fluttered open. Sara and Emma looked at each other then back down at Leila. Simultaneously the women shouted, "Yes!"

"What happened?" Leila asked in a distant voice.

"Lie still, everything is all right," Sara said, dabbing the corner of her eye with her shirtsleeve. "You are going to be just fine."

"Why am I lying on the ground?"

"We had the cart charging and you touched it. Must have been some sort of short circuit," Emma explained. "It damn near turned you into a crisp. You seriously kicked it. Sara brought you back."

"Don't you ever do something like that again," Sara said as tears streamed down her face.

Leila rubbed her chest. "I don't feel so good."

Sara heard the distinctive whine of an emergency vehicle getting closer. "Don't worry. Help is on the way."

The sound of the ambulance prompted Sara to ask Emma to tend to the two horses. They were content to occupy themselves eating grass along the edge of the driveway, but that would change as soon as the blaring van rolled up. Emma took their reins and hurried them into the safety of the barn, leaving Sara and Leila alone for a moment. Two out of three of the family's Great Danes started howling in tune with the wailing siren; Emma's smaller Fox Terriers fearlessly sprinted down the drive to face the noisy intruders.

"I heard you," Leila whispered. "You saved my life. I was almost gone. The light was right there, but you reminded me that I had to stay."

"Shh, we can talk about all that later."

The ambulance pulled to a stop about 10 feet away from the two old friends. A tall, bald man and a stout woman climbed out of the front seat. The woman rushed over to Leila as the man went around to the rear doors. "Hi. My name is Ann Marie and my partner is Frank," she said, dropping down to her knees next to Leila. She pulled a stethoscope from her bag, then asked, "Dispatch reported a case of seizures brought on by a powerful shock."

"Yes, then she stopped breathing. I started CPR and was able to bring her back right before you arrived," Sara replied, backing away to make room. She watched as Ann Marie listened to Leila's chest, then asked a number of simple questions to test for neurological damage.

As a blood pressure cuff was being strapped to Leila's arm, the other EMT arrived with the gurney. Ann Marie brought him up to speed by running through a list of medical stats.

"I guess you were meant to live another day," Frank said to Leila as he pulled out a pen light and looked into her eyes. "Pupils are reactive."

"BP is 105 over 68. All good, but you need to go to the hospital for further evaluation and monitoring," Ann Marie said with complete authority. "Let's get her up."

Frank nodded in agreement. In seconds, they had her strapped onto the gurney and were rolling it down the dirt drive to the back of the waiting ambulance.

"Sara, can you call Alex and tell him what happened?" Leila asked, straining to look behind her. "He should be at the vineyard."

"I'll call him now. And don't worry; I'll be following right behind you," Sara answered.

Just as Frank was stepping out the back of the ambulance to secure the rear doors, Leila called out. "Please, look after my puppy, too. She's in my car."

"Wait. Did you say puppy?"

The doors were locked before Sara could ask anything else.

~

A soft brush on her cheek shook Leila free from the dark void that her mind had fallen into as she dozed on an uncomfortable cot in the emergency room. Standing over her was a tall, well- built man with eyes the shade of the Pacific Ocean, a blue so deep that the color blended effortlessly into his inky pupils. A mix of silver and sandy hair fell to the back of his neck. He was smiling, but worry was clearly carved into all of his features.

"Hey, beautiful. There you are," Alex said, the smooth baritone of his voice unnaturally off key from fear.

"Hi. How long have you been here?" Leila asked.

"A little while. Sara phoned." Alex glanced at the slim woman leaning against the far wall. "She scared the hell out of me. I didn't know what I would find when I arrived."

"Sorry," Leila whispered, still groggy.

"Damn near had a heart attack on the drive over," he said, running his hand through his thick hair. "I was having palpitations the whole way. God, if I lost you...."

Leila smiled, recognizing how rattled he was by her situation.

He leaned over, bringing his face to within inches of hers, so he could stare directly into her eyes. "Swear to God that you'll never frighten me like that again."

Leila mouthed the word, "Promise."

Alex sighed heavily, kissed her on the forehead then straightened back up, not appearing the least bit comforted.

"How long was I out?" Leila asked, turning toward Sara. She felt as if she were surfacing from a narcotic-induced fog.

"You dozed off for about half an hour. The doctor said you will be pretty wiped out for the next few days," Sara answered. She was still in her tan britches and tall, leather boots. Her light brown hair was pulled back tightly into a neat pony tail.

"I guess the pain killer they gave me for the burns knocked me out. They had to take my ring off. Not a pleasant experience," Leila said, looking down at her bandaged left hand. "Where is it? Do you have it, Sara?"

"Don't worry. The nurse gave it to me," Alex said, producing the sparkling two-carat diamond ring from the front pocket of his jeans. "Let me slip it on your right hand for now. I don't want you to get used to having it off. Plus, it's more likely to get lost in my pants pocket." After sliding it down her finger, he gently pressed his lips against her hand.

Leila watched as tears swelled in the corners of his eyes, threatening to spill over.

"I can't wait to celebrate. As soon as you get back on your feet, we are popping the champagne," Sara said, cheerfully.

The image made Leila smile. "Sounds good."

"I never thought I would see the day when you agreed to walk down the aisle or, come to think of it, have a puppy," Sara continued.

"And look what it got me, almost killed," Leila replied weakly.

"Not funny!" The muscles along Alex's jaw-line

reflexively popped out as he scolded his fiancée. "You don't realize how close a call it was. I don't know whether to be furious at Sara about what happened or to kiss her for saving you…saving us."

Leila noticed Sara squirm uncomfortably in the corner of the room, then look at the floor.

"Accidents happen," Leila replied softly, but she couldn't help thinking about her near-death experience. She recalled white light radiating all around her, drawing her closer to its core. Leila intuitively knew everything would be all right; she was at peace. She was one step away from crossing over the threshold, permanently severing the connection to her physical existence, when Sara's voice seemed to penetrate her mind. Or was it her soul? Leila wasn't sure which, but in the end, that link tugged her back like a marionette.

"If I need to remind you, you're not a cat with lives to spare. One brush with the Grim Reaper is more than enough," Alex said authoritatively.

Leila squeezed his hand and nodded. *Damn, this really stinks. I want to be home. I wonder how long I'll be stuck in this place?* Leila thought.

Sara lifted her gaze from her feet and spoke. "The doctor said you'll be in the hospital for a few more days. A neurologist will stop by later to do more tests."

Surprised by her friend's words, Leila could only muster a blank stare. *"How the heck…?"*

"Oh, thanks. I haven't had a chance to talk to whoever is treating her," Alex said. "Maybe I should track the doc down before Sara leaves."

"Yeah, why don't you do that?" Leila suggested.

Alex kissed her on the forehead and disappeared from the tiny ER room. Leila could feel herself beaming as she watched him go.

"I'm so sorry," Sara said, coming over to sit on the bed.

"Please stop. It could have happened to anyone, including you," Leila replied. The gravity of the day's events weighed heavily on her thoughts, but something more was on her mind. Leila broke the momentary silence. "How did you do that?"

Sara looked perplexed. "Do what, CPR?"

"No. Two seconds ago I was wondering how long I would have to be in here, and then it was like you answered me. But I didn't say it out loud."

Sara blinked and hesitated. "I…I don't know. I guess I thought you wanted to know."

"Okay, that is just freakin' weird," Leila said. *Kind of like the whole damn day*, she added in her mind.

"Kind of like the whole day, huh?" Sara muttered.

Leila squinted and shook her head, not sure if she had heard her friend correctly. "What did you say?"

"Like the entire day. Why?"

"I was thinking the same thing." Leila didn't know what to make of it. She figured she must be reading too much into the coincidence. She had enough trouble focusing on her immediate reality, let alone some odd circumstance. But still, it made the back of her neck feel prickly.

"You really do love Alex, don't you?" Sara asked, changing the subject.

Leila nodded. "I'm not sure how it happened. I resisted the whole 'love thing' all these years, then bam! He had me hooked."

"Amen to that," Sara said. "He loves you in spite of you pulling out every trick in the book to push him away."

Leila smiled. "He does, doesn't he? I even told him about my strict rule: No guy is allowed to last longer than six months. Over the years, that adds up to quite a few. But he didn't care."

"I hear that red is the 'in' color for wedding dresses,"

Sara joked.

"It was always such a rush of adrenaline to set the limits with those powerful men. To be the one in control," Leila said.

"But were you happy?" Sara asked.

I always thought I was, but now.... Leila gazed at her two carat ring. "I'm not sure."

"Come on. I've known you since I was 10. There was no way that having some false sense of control could make up for the lack of love in your life. I'm so relieved that Alex saved you from yourself."

Leila closed her eyes and thought about this for a moment. Though Sara revived her body, it was Alex who warmed her heart, thawing it and bringing it back to life. When Leila opened them again, her fiancé was walking into the room. "Hey, did you find my doctor?"

"Yes, you'll be here for a few days while they monitor the residual effects of the accident, and then it's going to be back to the vineyard with me. He said you shouldn't be alone in case you develop some delayed cognitive issues. Frying your brain and nervous system isn't such a good thing," he explained.

No, I wouldn't expect that it is. Leila yawned. It was clear that even talking was taking its toll, plus her hand was starting to throb again. "All I care about right now is getting some more pain-killers and sleep."

"The doctor said he would be by to check on you in a few minutes," Alex said. "I'm sure he'll have a nurse give you another dose when he is done."

"Since your knight in shining armor is here, I'm going to run home," Sara said, giving her best friend a peck on the cheek. "I have this tiny puppy with a giant attitude raising hell at the farm. Seems she has the rest of the dogs rolling over and doing her bidding. You know, I still haven't heard the whole story on how you ended up with a dog. And seriously, what's with the name? Who's ever heard of a Westie called Fifi? I think the Poodle breeders have that one copyrighted or trademarked."

"I thought she needed a pooch," Alex chimed in. "The woman is in desperate need of unconditional love, and sometimes I can't be there."

Leila smiled and nodded. "And I like the name and that's all that matters."

"Leila and unconditional love, quite a match," Sara said, moving toward the door. "Don't get into any more trouble, okay? And you, take good care of my girl."

"Don't worry," Alex replied as Sara waved good-bye from the doorway. "I have her number. She lives by my rules now."

Leila's eyes darted over to his. A pang of anxiety shot through her fatigued and bruised muscles.

"Yeah, right…you go with that," Sara said, chuckling before trotting away.

CHAPTER TWO

Sara felt herself being shaken awake at 4:00 a.m. It had been three weeks since the accident with the golf cart, but she was still feeling the mental after-effects of the incident. It seemed like her dreams were consistently plagued by nightmares. David, her husband, was next to her, nudging her back from the cold, desolate darkness of tonight's episode. She was thankful.

"Sara, you were crying in your sleep again," David whispered.

She felt her cheeks and they were moist with tears. "Geez, I'm sorry I woke you. I don't know what's wrong with me."

"Maybe you should talk to a professional about this. I think Leila's brush with death has bothered you more than you're willing to admit," he said, reaching to his side to turn on a lamp.

"That's ridiculous. It wasn't me who died and came back to life. If anyone should be having issues like this, it should be Leila," Sara replied, fully awake now and staring at her husband.

"Yes, but my primary concern is you. Plus, who's to say she isn't a basket case? Have you asked her?"

"Not exactly," she replied.

Sara thought about the last conversation she had with Leila. They discussed how she was doing physically, but didn't really touch on what was happening psychologically. *Why?* she wondered. *I guess I already know.* The last few weeks weren't only filled with bad dreams; they were filled with flashes of intense emotions and thoughts, some that Sara sensed weren't her own. It reminded her of a childhood game of telephone, where two children held plastic cups connected by a long string. When one child whispered into the cup, the other could hear what was being said. Sara shivered under the covers.

"Honey, you saw your best friend stop breathing, right in front of you," David explained gently, adjusting his position to face her. "That had to leave a profound and traumatic mark. I won't even mention the ambivalence that might be connected to the announcement that she's getting married. Are you losing your pseudo-sister or gaining a pseudo-brother-in-law?"

"That is ridiculous," Sara replied. "I don't have any reservations about their marriage."

"Leila…married. The one who should be having nightmares is Alex," he teased.

"You're terrible. Alex is a lucky guy. He's the only man she has ever let us meet, so that has to say something about how serious she is about their relationship. She just had to find the right person to help her get over all the abandonment issues left over from her dad taking off." Sara frowned and poked him in the ribs. "But I get your point about the rest of it."

"Promise me you'll at least think about talking to someone about what's going on in that complicated head of yours," David said.

I don't think a shrink is going to be able to help with this problem. Sara thought. *A psychic maybe, but definitely not some run-of-the-mill counselor. I'd be on anti-psychotic medication before the end of the first session.*

David leaned over and kissed her on the forehead, then mouthed the word please.

"Okay, as long as you don't keep bugging me about it," Sara replied.

He smiled appreciatively and nodded.

Sara recalled something her best friend told her the last time they spoke. "Hey, I forgot to tell you about Leila's hair.

She chopped about eight inches off the ends because the accident left it so burned and frayed. Can you picture her without those long, dark locks?"

"Not really," David answered.

"Lucky for her it still covers that big funky birthmark on the back of her neck," she continued. "She's always been so self-conscious about anyone seeing it."

David's eyebrows narrowed into a serious expression. "Come to think of it, in all the years we've been together, I bet I've only seen her sporting a ponytail a handful of times. I don't know, Honey. It's like Leila's been transformed into a whole new person: new hair, new man, new dog, new attitude, second chance at life. No wonder you're freaking out. Your best friend has turned into someone you don't know," he said, with a smirk.

This time, Sara hit him in the face with a pillow. "Not funny."

"A little bit funny," he answered, trying to dodge the blow.

"Only to you," she said, clobbering him again.

The next morning Sara decided she was way too tired and mentally distracted to do anything other than saddle up Gale Force and go for a relaxing ride around the property. She tried clearing her head, but no matter what she did, her thoughts kept returning to Leila. The phone hooked on Sara's belt vibrated, breaking the trance she had fallen under. She briefly halted her horse to answer the call. *I'm not surprised*, she thought when she looked at the number. It was Leila.

"Hey, girl. How are you feeling?" Sara asked, urging her mount forward.

"I'm hanging in there. Less sore every day. You should be hearing from my lawyer any time now. I figure you'll be paying my mortgage by next month," she replied.

"I'm sure you'll be asking for my first born as part of the settlement," Sara joked.

"That's okay," Leila answered with a sigh. "You can keep Jack. He's 12, almost a teenager. I don't need that kind of trouble, even if he is the greatest kid on Earth. But I do want a couple of small favors laden with lots of guilt."

"This sounds like it is going to be a doozey. Lay it on me." Sara braced herself as she guided the Irish thoroughbred onto the path that ran around the perimeter of a large hay field.

"First, I wanted to ask you to be my matron-of-honor. I was going to ask you sooner, but my brain has been a little bit off lately. If you say no, I will have to hunt you down and hurt you. You're all I have," Leila said sadly.

"Of course!" Sara answered. "I would be crushed if you didn't ask me. And please, I know you have other friends."

"Name one," Leila replied.

"Emma."

"That's true. Emma and I did become pretty good friends after Jack's bad fall and that whole fiasco with your family. Maybe I'll ask her to be in the wedding too."

Sara recalled when her family first moved to the farm. They were only in the house for a couple of months when Sara's young son, Jack, sustained life-threatening injuries in a freak riding accident. He languished in a coma for days but thankfully, made a full recovery. Leila and Emma rarely left her side and were key allies in helping Sara decipher a number of unexplainable coincidences that contributed to the fall. When everything was finally pieced together, she uncovered a scandalous mystery that had been plaguing the estate for decades. It ultimately led to the discovery that Sara was born at the house and given up for adoption.

"Sara? Sara? Are you there? Do you hear me?" Leila asked, apparently concerned that the call was dropped.

"Sorry. I got lost in the past for a minute," Sara replied,

trying to shake off the feeling of being in danger, from whom or what, she wasn't quite sure.

"I'm not done extracting my pound of flesh from you, so refocus," Leila said with a laugh.

"Go on. What's next?"

As if on cue, a young buck popped up from his resting place behind some blackberry bushes, startling Sara's horse and reflexively propelling the gelding into flight. She squeezed her legs tightly against his sides to keep her balance as he reared up and bolted sideways.

"Whoa, fella," Sara said, calming the snorting animal with a pat on the shoulder. "Sorry. Minor equine distraction. Go on."

"You know how we've spent Thanksgiving together for the last 15 years?"

"I think I have a memory of that. I cook; you eat and get drunk. Why? Do you want to bring Alex? No problem. He's going to be family soon anyway."

Sara felt a surge of anxiety. She could feel her heart racing while her lungs tightened, restricting her airflow. She wondered if it was a delayed response to Gale Force's swift reaction, but a small voice in her head was telling her it was coming from another source – the woman on the other end of the call.

There was a brief pause before Leila's voice resonated over the line. "I actually had another plan in mind, something special. I want you, David and Jack to have dinner with us this Thanksgiving in Charleston. It's at Alex's mother's house. Please, please, please. You can't say no." She was practically begging.

"Are you nuts? You want us to go to your future mother-in-law's house? Does she even know about this?" Sara shook her head in disbelief over such a ridiculous idea.

"Alex convinced her that having you there would be a

great idea since you're the only family I care about, which you know is especially true since my mom had her mind-warping stroke two years ago. I pray I die if anything like that ever happens to me. I don't want to end up lingering in a nursing home."

"I have to agree with you there, but…," Sara ineffectively interjected.

Leila continued to rant on about her dysfunctional family. Sara listened patiently, but the rage coming across the phone was palpable. Sara thought back to the day she found 14-year-old Leila crying hysterically in the school bathroom. She was stunned when the distraught girl revealed through gut-wrenching sobs that her dad had moved out, leaving her and her mom so he could shack up with a woman barely passing as an adult. He left and never looked back, severing almost all contact and communication with his children. Sara always knew this sat at the core of Leila's complicated relationships with men; she wouldn't trust their word or risk having her heart broken.

"Hey, you still out there?" Leila asked.

Sara shook herself from her thoughts. "But you still have your brother, Royce," she suggested, trying to foster a semblance of a familial link.

"In case you haven't noticed, we fall painfully short when it comes to sibling bonding," Leila responded. "A 10 year age difference is hard to overcome in the best of circumstances. It didn't help that he split to San Francisco the moment they handed him his high school diploma. About all we have in common is our DNA and that we both like men."

"You're too tough on him. I think you should try harder. At least invite him to the wedding."

"We'll see. In the meantime, Ms. Sara, the Millers are all that matter in the family department. Have I mentioned that you saved my life and I told Alex I wouldn't go unless you came too?" Leila asked playfully, like a pouty child.

"You've got to be kidding," Sara said in total disgust. "You blackmailed Alex already? You, my dear, are a dark force with lots of unresolved issues."

"Come on," Leila said, ignoring the analysis. "It will be a cool trip. Charleston is absolutely beautiful. They have huge historic mansions, century-old trees with all that funky moss hanging down, not to mention the great antiques."

"And your future mother-in-law and father-in-law and whoever else make up the Whitfield clan," Sara replied. "Sorry, girl, but no thank you!"

"It will only be his mom, Constance, and Alex's younger brother, Maxim, and of course, the five of us. Alex's parents have been divorced almost as long as mine and she never remarried. I don't want to meet them all alone. What if they don't like me? And then he dumps me? Please, I need back-up."

Sara thought this was proof of it; the golf cart fried her friend's brain. The man clearly adored her and wouldn't give a damn what anyone else said, even his family. "You have nothing to be nervous about," she replied. "His folks are gonna love you. Plus, they're Southern; even if they totally hate your guts they'll be polite and gracious to your face."

"Please. You owe me," Leila said. "I know Alex loves me, I really do, but I've been having these awful dreams that are freaking me out. I don't think dying and coming back to life left me in a very good place mentally."

"What kind of dreams?" Sara asked, immediately thinking about her own recent bout with nightmares. The most frustrating part was that she could never remember the details. The only thing she was certain of was the feeling that someone or something was stalking her like an unpredictable and vicious predator.

"I'll tell you if you agree to Thanksgiving in Charleston,"

Leila said.

"If you spill your guts, I'll agree to ask David, but he may say no. I can't guarantee anything. Got it?"

"Deal." Leila let out a loud sigh before continuing with her story. "I'm worried that I might be trying to create a reason to run away from Alex. In these dreams, I'm trapped and unable to break free. I always have a sense that someone is playing with me, like a cat and mouse, torturing me before I'm killed. My God, even I can decipher this one! It's why I initiated the six month rule to begin with, so I could never get hurt. I'm worried that I'll sabotage our relationship if I get a hint that I could be right. But damn it! I don't want to do that. I want the happily ever after."

Sara's skin crawled as Leila seemed to climb inside her head. The likeness of the image of an unspecified danger and the emotions they evoked were too much of a disturbing coincidence. Sara was about to confess to Leila that she was having similar dreams, but hesitated when she sensed her friend was on the verge of tears. She didn't want to add any fuel to Leila's smoldering doubts or create a crack in the couple's newly poured foundation. Were they both having the same dream, or was Sara zeroing in on Leila's rattled unconscious, the way an antenna picks up a radio wave? She couldn't be certain, but the feeling that this was a bad omen settled into the back of her mind like an unwelcome guest. Either way, she didn't like it.

Sara tried her best to reassure her fragile friend. "I think you need to take a deep breath. You two are great together. You weren't giving into any of these insecurities before you got zapped. I'm sure this is one of those lingering repercussions the neurologist mentioned. "

Leila answered, with a sniffle, "I don't think it's neurological. I think I'm just a mental screw-up when it comes to any kind of serious relationship."

Sara had a hard time thinking of an argument for that point. She could feel Leila's pain through the phone. "Stop thinking like that. You deserve a happy ending."

"I hope you're right," Leila replied in a barely audible voice.

"About Thanksgiving, I'm sure David will say yes," Sara said, feeling suddenly protective of her old friend. And there was something else too, a sense that her blossoming mental connection to Leila was created for a reason. The only problem was that she didn't have a clue as to what that purpose could be. "You can count us in."

"You're the best!" Leila squealed.

"That's what a family is for. Any other requests while you have me feeling guilty and bad for your sorry butt?" Sara asked.

"That will do for now," Leila replied. "I'm going to call Alex with the news. We'll chat about the details soon. Thanks a bunch. Bye."

Sara snapped the phone back onto her belt, gave Gale Force's sides a small kick with her heels and trotted down the dirt path. Unfortunately she couldn't leave behind the sinking feeling that her world was shifting in an unseen and perilous way.

CHAPTER THREE

Winter was threatening to arrive early. Snowflakes the size of silver dollars dotted the November sky as the mercury in the thermometer pushed below 30 degrees Fahrenheit. Sara was bundled up in a heavy wool coat and scarf. She shoved her chilled fingers deep into her pockets as she braced for the walk down the cemetery path. Seasonal mums were placed next to quite a few of the headstones. The sight of the yellow and orange blooms gnawed at the back of Sara's conscience. She absentmindedly forgot to bring anything, but then again, she was really here to take, not to give. A fountain topped by a mournful angel gazed down at her as she passed. Its water trickled tenaciously in spite of the frigid weather.

Within a few yards, Sara found what she was searching for; the grave of her biological mother, Kathleen McHugh. Customarily, she avoided the graveyard, even after her brother lured her into attending Mass on Sundays. She wasn't exactly sure what she was hoping to achieve by coming now. The snow was quickly accumulating on cold surfaces, and the granite markers were no exception. Sara pulled out a gloved hand and brushed off the Celtic pattern carved into the stone. Its intricate curves reminded her of the meaning young Kathleen, or Katy, ascribed to it, that a family is bound together through this never-ending line that twists and turns but never breaks. Eventually, it folds back and repeats itself over again, like being reborn or given a chance at redemption. When Sara first heard this, it was oddly comforting, but today, it only made her shiver. *I don't understand this telepathy thing I seem to be developing. My intuition is telling me to be very careful, but I don't know why.*

"Help me," Sara said aloud. "You did before. Why are

these strange things happening?"

"What things?" a deep male voice asked.

She jumped about a foot in the air and spun around to find her fraternal twin, Father Thomas O'Connor. The siblings were separated at birth and placed into adoptive homes in different states. They didn't even know of each other's existence until a few years ago. Since the surprising revelation about their connected identity, their relationship had grown like a honeysuckle vine in bloom, spreading with abandon, constantly intertwining.

"Jesus, Thomas! Are you trying to drum up business?"

"It's a sin to say the Lord's name in vain," he scolded, shooting a reproachful look at her as she rolled her eyes. Icy white flecks clung to his black hair, accentuating his priestly attire. "That will be five Hail Marys for you. You didn't answer my question," he continued, stepping forward to make the sign of the cross in front of their mother's grave. "What odd things are troubling you now?"

Sara opened her mouth but nothing came out. She didn't know how to explain and she wasn't sure she wanted to.

"You haven't even spoken and already I don't like the sound of it." He skillfully pinned her down with his intense blue eyes.

"Long story," she replied.

"That's the thing about priests; we're trained to listen. Come inside, I'll whip you up a hot chocolate. If you say your Hail Marys first, I'll even throw in some mini-marshmallows."

Sara knew she was defeated. She looped her arm through his as they walked back to the parish house. "Cookies too?"

"I'm sure I can dig a few up," he said, grinning like a mischievous kid.

Once inside the kitchen, she watched in awe as Thomas worked his magic the old fashioned way, whisking together a delectable froth of powdered chocolate, sugar, milk and vanilla. He poured the creamy mixture into two large mugs, topped them with whipped cream and tiny marshmallows then sprinkled a little cocoa powder on top. Then, as promised, he filled a plate with a mouth-watering array of homemade cookies.

Sara helped him carry their goodies to the table. The smell was intoxicating. She took a sip and then licked the foam off her lips. "This is so good, it's sinful."

"Mmm, I have to agree," he said with a smile. He picked up a sugar cookie and waved it in his sister's direction. "Tell me. What has you asking Katy for help?"

"Bad dreams to start, but there's more, I think something happened to me, or us, when I saved Leila's life. I think balancing on the edge of death's threshold opened a door, or rather a channel…a psychic one. I know it sounds stupid, but I thought Katy might give me a sign or guidance of some sort." Sara stuffed one of the baked treats in her mouth and shrugged.

"Hmm, it would be better to start from the beginning," he suggested, sounding worried. "Maybe I can help."

Sara detailed all the troubling coincidences since the day Leila was electrocuted. "We've been friends for so long that we know each other inside and out, but now…well, I seem to have developed a direct line into her thoughts and feelings. Don't get me wrong, it's not like I'm constantly eavesdropping. The experience more closely resembles when a stray conversation is picked up on your cell phone. I will hear her voice in my head or see a flash of what she is seeing, or maybe thinking. I'm not completely certain. Lately I've started paying attention, and it seems to be particularly strong whenever she's having a powerful emotion."

Thomas listened intently, interrupting once or twice for clarification. By the time she was done, they had wolfed down everything but a single gingersnap.

"And Leila, does she seem normal to you?" he asked.

"That's all relative. She hasn't acted like Leila since Alex came into her life. So in one way she's behaving unusually, but in another, she's acting healthier."

"I see your point, but that wasn't exactly what I was trying to tease out. Does this flow of information only go in one direction, or is she receiving random messages from you as well?"

Sara considered this for a moment. It hadn't even crossed her mind that her thoughts could be broadcast the other way. She never mentioned anything to Leila. It seemed like the poor girl had enough on her plate with the engagement and her recovery. "To be honest, I haven't shared any of this with her yet. I guess I should."

Tom looked at her thoughtfully before he spoke. "Leila was close to crossing into the light of God's grace but was pulled back to her physical existence at the last moment by you, someone who has already shown a heightened sensitivity to the paranormal. I imagine that this surge in activity points to some kind of open conduit, possibly one leading to the other side."

"Ah, geez," Sara said. *That's the last thing I need.*

"It would be best to tread lightly," Thomas suggested, adding to his theory. "Everything could get ratcheted up when you're in each other's company."

"Just perfect."

Sara realized that she hadn't actually been in Leila's presence since her friend was released from the hospital. At that time, she chalked everything up to sheer coincidence. *Not anymore. We're going to have to get a handle on this, and fast. Damn.*

"So what do you suggest?" Sara asked. "We test it out? Personally, I much prefer to shut it down; you know, flip the switch. Leila's my best friend. I'm her matron-of-honor. We're not about to move to opposite sides of the country. So come on, tell me how to turn it off. "

Thomas sighed, lifted his mug and finished off the last drop of his cocoa. "I don't have any idea how to accomplish that, but don't underestimate the power of prayer."

"Great," Sara said sarcastically.

Thomas seemed to ignore his twin's tone of voice and continued. "Beyond that, I think you need to find an expert on the subject; someone knowledgeable about the steps required to control your gift safely."

Sara felt more anxious than when she arrived at the cemetery. She thought back to promising David she would find a "professional" to talk to. Now it appeared that her brother was encouraging a similar course of action.

"The real test will be when you and Leila are together. If your abilities are magnified, you risk the possibility of attracting earth-bound souls, and not all of them are benign. Please do me a favor. Find a mentor, someone you can call if you find you're in over your head. You have some experience. Katy needed you to bring closure. Even though she didn't mean to do any harm, Jack almost died in a replay of your farm's tragic history. Imagine if a spirit is purposefully coming over to cause suffering...or worse."

Sara was quiet for a while as she finished her drink. So many thoughts crowded her brain that it made her want to pull the top off her skull to make room. "You're right. I need to be the one in charge. There's the possibility that this won't pass. Hell, I could be stuck like this for good! I can't risk it."

"Keep me updated," he said, squeezing her hand. "I'll help in any way I can."

Help. That's exactly what I need. Sara recognized an opportunity when it came knocking. She smiled. "Tom, you've given me an idea. How would you like to take a trip into Leesburg this week to visit Leila?"

He looked at her suspiciously. "What are you plotting?"

Sara figured that having third party verification that the entire phenomenon wasn't a terrible hallucination would be a good idea. She went on to suggest a way to test her new ability with his assistance. After getting his reluctant agreement, Sara glanced out the window. The snow had picked up while the siblings were inside talking.

"I better get going before it gets any worse out there," she said.

Tom nodded as they rose. "Call me tonight and I'll let you know which day will work best."

When Sara opened the front door of the parish house, she was surprised to see the ground covered in a glittering white frosting a couple of inches thick.

She couldn't resist commenting about the wintery scene. "Beautiful but dangerous."

"I'll walk you out. I need to run over to my office anyway." He followed her down the steps.

"I meant to ask, have you talked to Sean?" Sara asked.

After retiring a couple of years ago, their biological father, Sean, organized a trip of a lifetime. He was spending close to eight weeks touring most of Europe and then was scheduled to take a Mediterranean/trans-Atlantic cruise home. Thomas dropped him off at the airport a few days ago and he wouldn't arrive back in the States until early January.

"Yes, he called when he landed in Ireland," Tom answered. "He was in Dublin raising a pint or two. By now, he should be in London. I'm jealous. It sounded like he was having a big time."

"I'm glad," Sara said, unlocking the driver's door. "Thanks for the ear and the advice. I'll be in touch."

Thomas watched her climb behind the wheel. "Anytime.

Be careful out there, it's becoming a bit treacherous."

Sara nodded and then started the engine. As she made the turn out of the parking lot, her tires lost traction, precariously whipping the vehicle across the slick road. The driver of an oncoming truck laid on his horn and swerved, barely missing her car. Adrenaline surged through her body like flood water breaching a dam. After barely averting an accident, Sara re-established control and cautiously proceeded on her way.

~

Leila tapped her perfectly manicured cherry-red nails on the one remaining open space of her cluttered desk. Piled carelessly to her right was a multitude of expensive fringes and tassels; to the left, a small mountain of fabric samples. Immediately in front of her was a teetering stack of trade magazines, topped by the most recent edition of *Modern Bride*. A frigid, half-finished latte and barely nibbled stale croissant were squeezed into a corner of the mess. Fifi was soundly snoozing on a round cushion at her feet. The sound of the telephone ringing briefly caught her attention, but she ignored it, a pattern she repeated all day long.

The shop had opened on time at ten o'clock that morning. Leila sent her assistant, Gabrielle, home at five after ten. She needed time alone, which translated into a paid day off for Gabbie. The world was full of surprises, even for the hired help. *Life is about maneuvering through some radical and unexpected turns,* Leila thought. Unfortunately, she was feeling more and more like she was speeding down the Pacific Coast Highway with locked-up power steering and no brakes. The closer happiness came to being within reach, the more she was convinced that she was about to crash through the safety barrier and plunge headlong onto the merciless rocks below.

Today, it was the first phone message on her answering machine that had Leila convinced that her fragile little world was on the verge of blowing apart in a spectacular fashion. The sound of her father's voice made her furious. *I need to think. I just need to dispose of this one small problem and everything will be back on track. Nobody is going to screw that special day up for me, especially not that sorry son of a....*

The tinkle of the brass bells tied to the shop's front door roused her from her state of concentration. Fifi jumped to attention and poked her head up, gauging whether the intruder was a friend or foe. Leila saw someone hidden behind a closing umbrella. As the drenched black fabric collapsed on itself, she recognized her visitor – Sara's brother, Father Thomas O'Connor. Fifi issued a snort of acceptance, then returned to her bed.

"Father Tom, to what do I owe the pleasure?" Leila asked, rising to give him a hug and a kiss on the cheek.

"Afternoon, Leila," the soggy priest replied. "I was in Leesburg on charity business and thought I would swing by to see how you're holding up with the wedding arrangements. Sara stopped by the church a few days ago, which gave us a chance to catch up. She says you're full steam ahead."

Leila smiled. "Isn't she the efficient publicist?"

"She can be, but to be honest, I think she's been troubled lately," he said, his tone turning more serious.

This piqued Leila's curiosity. Sara hadn't mentioned anything specific to her, but she couldn't shake a feeling that Sara was hiding something. "What do you mean?"

"Actually, she asked me not to say anything, so I was hoping you already knew," he replied, looking away. "It wouldn't be a breach of confidence in that case."

"I'm not exactly sure what you're referring to, but since she's my best friend, as far as I'm concerned, to hell with privacy. Tell me what's wrong." Leila was beginning to get nervous.

Tom gazed silently at Leila for a moment, but then shifted his focus to the ground.

She could tell he was uncomfortable and stalling. *Uh-oh. Whatever it is must be serious.*

"How about you? Anything out of the ordinary?" he asked, shoving his hands deep into his coat pockets.

"Other than almost dying and getting married, nothing at all," Leila answered smartly, feeling completely frustrated by the change of subject. "Come on, Tom. What's going on?"

"Well, it's David," he replied, keeping his focus toward the floor. "Sara found him with another woman."

Leila felt like she was slapped across the face. She had to force herself to breathe. "No. It can't be. I don't believe it."

"I know, it's hard to imagine," Tom half-whispered.

"Sara must be completely devastated," Leila said, feeling sick to her stomach. "I knew she was hiding something the last few weeks. Oh my God, are they getting a divorce? Poor Jack!"

She brought her hand to her mouth as tears welled up in the corners of her eyes. *He's going to grow up in a broken family, just like I did. Why the heck didn't she tell me? I should have been there for her. Didn't she think I could handle it?* Leila recalled a passing sense that Sara was protecting her from something. *But this? Then again, I always considered them the perfect couple. Damn, if they can't make it, Alex and I don't have a fighting chance.* Anger, sorrow, and a bit of growing panic expanded exponentially in her chest.

A buzzing noise interrupted her thoughts. Tom retrieved his cell phone from his pocket.

"Sorry, I need to take this," he said, stepping away to talk to whomever was on the other end of the line. He turned his back toward Leila, apparently trying to create a bit of privacy.

Shell-shocked, Leila went back to her chair and sat down. She watched the priest nod several times and quietly say "yes" and "exactly". There was something oddly guarded in his demeanor that made her suspicious. When she spotted Sara walking up the sidewalk with a phone pressed to her ear, Leila didn't know what to make of it.

"Hi, Lei," Sara said as she entered the shop. A guilty expression was plastered across her face as she shook the rain droplets from her jacket. "We need to talk to you."

Leila realized that her friend wasn't surprised by her brother's presence. In fact, she didn't even acknowledge him. *She must have called Tom and he told her he spoke to me about the divorce. She has to be feeling kind of awkward.*

"Sara, why didn't you tell me about David?" Leila asked, standing up.

"Because it isn't true," Sara answered, sheepishly. "Tom made it up so we could test a theory. But please don't be mad until you hear me out."

"What?" Leila replied, stunned. *Alright, I'm completely confused.*

"I needed him to get a big emotional reaction from you, so I could be sure. I didn't know in advance what he was going to say, but from your response…your thoughts and feelings…I now know what he told you: David was cheating on me and we're splitting up. It got you pretty pissed off, but it also made you really sad. "

Leila was trying to sort through what Sara was saying, but none of it made any sense. "Huh? So he didn't have an affair? Let me get this right: The two of you are just messing with my head for the fun of it?"

"I'm so sorry," Tom blurted out, making eye contact for the first time since he arrived. "I hated deceiving you.

Please, I'm certain you'll understand. It's actually quite remarkable."

"No," Sara interjected, stepping closer. "I swear we didn't do this for our amusement or as a trick or anything like that. Honest,"

"You have about two seconds to explain," Leila said impatiently. She was incredibly irritated, but a stronger emotion was gaining footing. Fear.

Sara took a deep breath, then summarized what she had been seeing and hearing for the last month, the culmination of which was the experiment involving Tom. She pointed to specific examples that were hard to call into question.

Leila pictured Sara as having some sort of antennae sticking out the top of her head. The whole idea of someone having unrestricted access to her inner thoughts made her shiver. "So you can read my mind? I'm not sure if I'm blown away with amazement or simply creeped out beyond belief. Actually, I'm not even one hundred percent convinced it's true."

Sara shrugged and nodded, clearly having dealt with a similar reaction.

"I'm surprised you feel that way after your brush with death," Tom said. "Many survivors come back believing they've tapped into their sixth sense."

"Not me. My experiences are simply the bleed-off from Sara's on-again-off-again relationship with the paranormal. I suspected she was hiding something from me because she was, not because she clued me in telepathically."

Thomas crinkled up the skin between his eyebrows and pushed his glasses up higher on the bridge of his nose. The priest was contemplative and quiet for a moment, making Leila even more uncomfortable in her own skin.

"Are you sure?" Sara asked. "It's very possible that it flows both ways. Up until today, you wouldn't have known what to make of fragmented messages. I haven't had anything major going in my life, so the frequency may be too low to hear. Plus, you could be less sensitive to it."

Leila gave Sara a stone cold look. "You've lost your marbles. Bad enough you have some funky psychic gift; don't be trying to pass it off on me. As a matter of fact, I would appreciate it if you could leave me out of this all together. Go listen in on somebody else's warped psyche."

"I'm not doing it on purpose," Sara protested defensively. "It's not like I have a choice; I can't put on a pair of telepathic-noise canceling headphones."

Leila was completely unnerved. The quickest and easiest way to deal with the situation was to change the subject and push it, no them, away. "I'm sorry. I have an awful lot on my plate right now. Whipping a wedding together, even a relatively small one, is no easy feat. As you can see, I'm buried under decisions while still trying to run my business. There's just no more room on my calendar, especially for this kind of wacky stuff. I would appreciate it if we could drop this. It was nice seeing the two of you, but I really need to get back to work."

Tom tugged on his sister's arm. "Yes, of course. I can see where you're coming from. There's only so much any one person can handle. You go back to what you were doing. Come on, Sara."

Sara scowled but then gave in. "Fine."

"Thanks." Leila walked them to the door.

The rain outside was coming down in silver sheets, quickly melting the snow into slushy puddles. The priest snapped open his umbrella and waited for his stubborn sibling to join him under its protective shell.

"Go start the car, Tom. I'll be right there," Sara said, nudging him forward.

He frowned, but then nodded and ran to the dated sedan

parked a few spaces away.

Leila exhaled loudly. "Now what?"

Sara sighed. "I know you don't want this to be true, I didn't want to believe it either, but unfortunately it is. I made an appointment to see a psychic. Maybe she can tell me what to do to make it go away," Sara answered. As she left the shelter of the shop, she offered some final advice. "In the meantime, call your father back. I know you've been avoiding it all day. Don't get married with that stuff muddling your brain. It will only trip you and Alex up later on."

Leila felt as if she was punched in the gut. "How…?" she started to reply.

Sara cocked her head to the side. "You know how."

Tom beeped, prompting Sara to turn and run for the car. Leila watched them drive a short way down the road and then vanish into the dense fog.

What a long stinkin' day, was the first thought to cross Leila's mind when she heard the clock behind her chime twice for half-past the hour, in this case, four-thirty. The second was, *It will be a cold day in hell when I call him back. You're wrong, my friend.* But even Leila couldn't discount everything Sara claimed; the revelations were too accurate for this phenomenon to be brushed aside as a sheer coincidence. For the first time, Leila seriously considered the possibility that she might have been ignoring the obvious. Goosebumps crawled across her skin. The prospect of being telepathic, even only a little bit, was making her feel like a character in a B-rated horror flick. She rubbed her heavy eyelids. Two bites of food and an early jolt of caffeine left her depleted. The added stress heaped on by her so-called good friends didn't help matters. Leila grabbed her purse, tucked the bridal magazine under one arm, Fifi under the other and called it quitting time.

CHAPTER FOUR

Sara drove to Old Town Alexandria a few days before the scheduled trip to Charleston, South Carolina. It was the direct result of a successful internet search of paranormal practitioners. Ava Duprey's bio listed her as a clairvoyant and psychic. Sara had no idea what the difference was, but apparently there was one. After considering the irrefutable results from her experiment with Tom and Leila, Sara decided not to waste any time in getting a professional opinion. She decided to keep the knowledge of this rendezvous with directory assistance to the other side from her husband. David would either discount the woman as a charlatan or be incensed that his wife was playing with hellfire.

Old Town looked pretty much how it sounded, complete with pre-Revolutionary colonial homes and quaint storefronts, cobblestone streets and an historic port. The city boasted everything, from rowdy pubs to trendy cafés; unique boutiques to upscale clothing chains; art and antique shops to two-story Federal style homes turned into high-powered law offices. With the sagging economy relying on robust and extended Christmas sales, November took on a new sparkle. The place was lovely any time of year, but the holiday season seemed to possess it, giving it a breathtaking charm and beauty. Traditional greens were hung with abandon and candles adorned every window.

Sara preferred to stroll along the bedecked sidewalks for almost any other reason than the one that brought her to town that day. She passed her location once or twice before finding an open parking space along a side street. Sunshine cut through the cloud cover, exposing the elusive blue sky. It seemed as if the entire month had been one prolonged, bleak storm. Sara zipped her coat as she counted down the numbers to her destination. A red brick building with black shutters and a lacquered door to match stood firm, waiting for her arrival. Above the entrance was a scrolled piece of iron-work with a rectangular wooden sign, which creaked arthritically with the biting winter wind. Ava Duprey's name and the title "Psychic" were painted above a rendition of a cloudy crystal ball. Sara rolled her eyes, imagining David's voice saying *"A complete sham. I told you so."* She checked her watch before knocking. The appointment was for two o'clock, but it was only ten till the hour. Sara was tempted to do some window-shopping until her allotted time, but the decision was pre-empted by a short middle-aged woman throwing open the door.

"You must be Sara Miller. I've been expecting you. I'm Ava." She motioned for Sara to come in.

Sara glanced at the two sets of windows that faced the street. Wooden slats extended three-quarters of the way up the interior of the original glass, making it unlikely that this small woman saw her standing on the stoop. *Chalk one up for Ava*, she thought.

"Thank you. I'm a little early, I hope you don't mind," Sara replied, following her into the bowels of the townhouse.

"If I did, I wouldn't have come out to get you."

Sara flipped through a quick mental checklist of what she thought a fortune-telling, ghost-whispering professional would look like: funky, gypsy skirt with a matching fringe-trimmed head scarf: Ava wore only blue jeans and a multi-colored, alpaca sweater. Dangling earrings: yup, gold with multi-colored beads that, surprisingly, coordinated with what she was wearing. Long, gray streaked hair: kind of. Ava had the salt-n-pepper thing going on, but the cut resembled a suburban queen's signature, a shoulder-length bob. Dark, mesmerizing eyes: not on this ghost guru. They were more like plain-Jane hazel with perfectly plucked brows. No broomsticks, candles or crystals. The place looked more like a comfy waiting room at a spa.

Ava turned to face her guest. "Most people are surprised the first time they visit a psychic. They expect us all to fit into some preconceived Hollywood mold. The reality is that we come from all religious backgrounds and ethnicities. We're as varied as the rest of the population. The gift goes to those who are sensitive to vibrations and open to listening to the still, small voice. It cuts across cultures and lifestyles."

Sara was caught off guard. Did Ava know what she was thinking? She nodded and smiled.

"Have a seat," Ava said, pointing to one of two chairs in the parlor. "When we spoke on the phone, you said you needed help understanding what is happening between you and a friend."

"Yes, that is right," Sara replied.

"But the energy in your silence also told me that you're struggling with understanding your own experiences. Yes?"

"I guess you could say that," Sara answered. "It started a couple of years back."

"When you moved to Virginia, you started paying attention to the energy, but it was there before. As a child, do you remember seeing things that others didn't notice or knowing things before they happened?"

Sara tried to dust off long forgotten memories from when she was a small girl. "No, not really, but I do recall I didn't like the dark. I never wanted to go to sleep."

"Where is your left hand right now?" Ava nodded toward the armrest.

Sara looked down at her hand then back at the small woman. "Um, attached to my arm?"

"Yes, obviously, but see how you have it draped over the side? What do you feel in your fingertips?" she asked. "Close your eyes and clear your head of everything but the sensations in your hand. Relax as you exhale."

Sara did as she was told. She concentrated, feeling the blood pump through each digit. She slowed her breathing, making a point of blowing out through her mouth, when suddenly it happened: her palm lifted, as if being pushed up. Shocked, she opened her eyes.

"What did you sense?" Ava asked.

"I'm not sure," Sara answered.

Satisfied, Ava smiled. "How did you get over the fear of the dark?"

A grainy scene from Sara's childhood popped into her head, something that had escaped her conscious thought for decades. "The dog," Sara said, astonished. "The big dog would come and lie by my bed at night. I would put my hand on his head and fall asleep. He wouldn't let anything come close. But he was a fantasy. I made him up."

"You would like to believe that, but no, he is one of your spirit guardians. He stays close to you, and that is what you just felt. He is sprawled out next to your chair now."

"No way," Sara replied, balking at such a far-fetched idea.

"That source of comfort and security spilled over to your physical life. As an adult, you physically surround yourself with large dogs."

Sara nodded, realizing this was true. "Great Danes."

"As a child, you didn't know what the vibrations meant or how to control them. The shadows were too dense and their outlines had too much form, so they frightened you. It's understandable. What came through, you tuned out. The gift became more and more distant. That reaction is more common than you would imagine. Children's sensitivities are magnified, but parents insist there are no such things as ghosts. As a person matures, psychology tells us that if you hear or see things that others can't, you must be crazy.

You joined the denial chorus. By moving here, the energy was concentrated and directed. It forced you to pay attention again."

"That would be putting it mildly," Sara said with a sarcastic edge. "My son, Jack, almost died. I didn't have a choice."

Ava leaned forward, touched Sara's arm and sighed. "Your son also has the gift. It was more vibrant when he was younger; like you, he stopped listening. The physical world obscures the spiritual world."

Sara recalled Jack's comments when he came out of the coma, how he reported watching from the other side as she discovered her own mother's grave.

"It will come back to him when he's ready, just like it's coming back to you," Ava said. "This time, the vibrations are swirling around your friend and they confuse you."

"Yes, my best friend, Leila. That's the reason why I'm here," Sara replied, wanting to get back on track. "I told you what she went through at my farm and what has been happening ever since: the emergence of a telepathic link. I'm hoping it will fade away on its own."

"If you really thought that, you wouldn't be here."

"I guess not," Sara said, feeling her pulse quicken.

Ava closed her eyes, inhaled deeply and sat very still. Both of her feet were flat on the ground, and her fingers curled around the end of the seat cushion as if she was bracing for impact. After what seemed like minutes, the woman exhaled and spoke.

"I'm not sure her soul wanted to stay with her physical body. She almost left, but your magnetic energy was hard to resist. There is a very powerful connection that binds the two of you together. This bond wound tighter after you revived her. Picture it as listening to the same radio station even though the two of you are in different locations; the instant Leila's spirit re-entered her body, a parallel network was forged. Crossing over to the other side, even briefly, heightened Leila's sixth sense. The psychic link that you share has branched out as if being fertilized by your combined energy. This direct line becomes active when one of you has a strong emotional reaction."

"So it does go both ways?" Sara asked. "I knew it. I suspected Leila could access my mind, but she flat out denied it."

"The energy hasn't been strong enough for her to recognize it as separate from her own thoughts. She was not born with heightened sensitivity; it was created during her accident. It makes sense that she would be more skeptical and less inclined to pay attention, but that doesn't make it any less real. When the critical time comes, she will hear."

Sara thought about Ava's words, *"When the critical time comes,"* what does that mean? How about figuring out how to control the volume before it ever gets to that level? Or better, get rid of it completely?

"Is there a way to turn it off?" Sara asked. "Frankly, I'm not so thrilled about getting regular updates about Leila's emotional state. I love her, but I would prefer to live without the intrusion."

"There are ways to tone it back, but accepting the gift will help you to use it when it is required most. I sense danger ahead for your friend. Keep track of what you perceive; it will pave the way to safety. There is movement on the other side; a presence shifting and manipulating energy to bring together a cast of unlikely characters. You will find yourself questioning the reality of the situation as it unfolds, but you must bide your time and wait to intervene. The conclusion needs to be allowed to unfurl in order for the cosmos to be satisfied."

Sara suddenly felt seriously under-qualified. "Could you

be more specific: any names, locations, hints about what I should be watching for? Telling me a mischievous spirit is hanging around somewhere between the physical world and our final destination, while moving folks about like pawns on a chess board, doesn't help me when I don't have any clue what I can do to defuse the situation. I may as well throw in the towel and say 'uncle' right now."

"Allow your power to mature," Ava advised her. "Become accustomed to listening for true distress. Your mind will learn to sort through the broadcasts; it will discriminate on the basis of what is important versus the static of background noise."

Sara felt her heart leap forward like a sprinter at the starting line in the Olympics. It was pounding so quickly she thought she might faint. *This is way beyond my scope. I'm never going to be able to do this. What if I screw up and Leila gets hurt, or worse?*

Ava didn't seem to notice Sara's slip into panic; either that or she was choosing to ignore it altogether. "At the same time, Leila needs to surround herself with light," Ava continued. "Help her to find her psychic inner core. Meditate. Bring the light out and around her, like a force field. Help her to call on her spirit guides and guardians. You need to do the same."

"How the heck do I do that?" Sara snapped.

"The same way I am telling you to do it," Ava explained, patiently. "Meditate, spend time concentrating on clearing your mind. Out of the peaceful silence, embrace the ever present force that embodies your core. Allow this seed of God to expand and spill around you. When you can do it, teach Leila. Ask for help and be ready to accept it. Don't delay."

Sara shuddered. "What if I can't?"

"You will," Ava said with a reassuring smile.

Sara wished she felt a fraction as confident about the situation. A clock on the mantle chimed three o'clock, signaling the end of their appointment. Sara opened her handbag and pulled out a check to cover the $85 fee.

When they started toward the front entrance, Ava broached another subject. "Always remember the power of the truth goes hand in hand with the power of forgiveness. That will need to be sorted out in the end."

"Super! The last time I ran into problems with the truth being hidden all hell broke loose."

"In a way, deceit is an evil noose; once ensnared, it is hard to untangle," Ava said. At the door, she offered her reluctant apprentice a final piece of advice. "Believe in your abilities and the overwhelming strength of your connection. It will be vital. If you don't, there can only be one ending. Faith will be a healing force."

Sara left feeling worse than when she arrived. When she got back to the car, she flipped open her cell phone and dialed Leila's number. When the answering machine picked up, she debated leaving a message, but ultimately listened to her gut. The conversation couldn't wait.

"Hi Leila, it's me. I know you're still angry about the other day with Tom, but we need to talk and I'm not taking 'no' for an answer. I'm on my way over. See you in 45 minutes."

She ended the call, then started the engine.

CHAPTER FIVE

Leila was the last person to climb into Alex's SUV at five o'clock in the morning the day before Thanksgiving. She was struggling with a case of overactive nerves that left her running back to the house multiple times for various things she forgot to pack. After 10 minutes of false starts, she squeezed her body in next to Jack in the backseat. Leila came to an uneasy truce with Sara about their unusual bond after her best friend showed up at her shop a couple of days earlier filled with dire warnings of doom if she didn't agree to start taking the situation seriously. Leila reluctantly agreed to discuss it more after the trip to South Carolina, but threatened Sara with ex-communication if she even hinted at it over the long weekend.

She glanced around the vehicle, briefly locking eyes with Sara, as they got underway. *At least I'm safe for the next 9 hours or so. You wouldn't dare to bring it up while the guys and Jack are crammed in here with us.*

The miles ticked by slowly as the two men sat up front, talking about Virginia's blossoming wine business, corporate espionage and a wide range of sports. Jack either played a portable electronic game or slept. Sara was unusually quiet, which was fine with Leila. She had enough conversation going on in her own head, her anxiety ratcheting up with each passing hour. It was four o'clock when they finally entered Charleston's historic district. Leila's stomach churned with a bubbling mix of emotions, including joyful relief over the torturous ride coming to an end and a stifling fear over meeting her fiancé's family for the first time.

Alex, on the other hand, appeared as cool and composed as could be, acting like a polished tour guide as he pointed out the highlights of the colonial city to his passengers as they all made their way to his mother's home on Church Street. "On your left is the old Charleston Market. There are lots of funky trinkets to buy down there, in addition to handmade jewelry and some really beautiful and unique baskets woven by a small army of highly skilled African-American women. On either side of the market you'll find a string of restaurants, ranging from casual to fine-dining, sweet shops with candy and ice cream. Other stuff too, but it's been a long time since I've been down there. It's become more of a tourist destination in the past 20 some years."

"How long has it been since you've lived here?" Sara asked.

"Since college, I guess," he answered.

Isn't that when we all make our escape? Leila thought.

Jack pointed to a line of carriages parked about a block down from where their car had slowed to a virtual crawl. "Mom, look at all the horses."

Leila rolled her eyes as she listened to Jack try to convince his mother that they should go for a carriage ride. *You live on a farm filled with horses, for goodness sake.*

"The tours are very popular, loaded with information. The driver describes the architecture, how the city was created and the role it had in American history. Other than my mother, it is probably the best source of Charleston's history that you can find," Alex explained.

"Alex's mom has lived here all her life. Their house has been in the family since the late 1700s," Leila added.

"No kidding? Does that mean the two of you will be moving to Charleston in years to come?" David asked.

"I don't see that happening. I'm very content in Virginia. Let's be honest; I'm much too happy playing in the dirt with my vines," Alex replied with a crooked smile directed at his fiancée. "My brother, Maxim, is much more at home here. He drinks up the extravagant, well-heeled social life, getting off on the status of being a descendent of one of the more successful settlers, which to me only means that they were lucky enough not to starve to death or die from a mosquito-borne illness before producing the next generation. Maxim takes it all too seriously. I sometimes wish I had been around for him more, a grounding influence, especially after the divorce, but I was young and only thinking about my own life back then. Ah, the things I would do differently, if I could only go back in time."

"Amen to that, brother," David said.

Leila could definitely relate. She could think of a long list of "do-over" moments. She had become the very woman that she cursed as a teenager, the one that tore families apart without a second thought or a hint of remorse. She recalled spending far too many nights dreaming up ways to extract revenge on the cold-hearted bitch that stole her father's love and affection. It shattered her mother's life…and hers too. She said a silent prayer of forgiveness as the hair on the back of her neck crawled with a sense of foreboding. She wondered whether she was given this second chance at life as an amazing present, to heal, and in the process, be able to seize real love and happiness. But then Leila shuddered as she considered an alternative possibility that Alex was sent to her as punishment, to let karma dole out one serious heart-breaking slap in the face.

"We're here," Alex announced as he slowed the SUV down in front of an impressive four-story home.

"Your family must be loaded," Jack commented. "Then again, it seems like everyone we know is rich, well except Emma of course."

"Zip it, Jack," Sara warned. "You're being rude."

Jack rolled his eyes and turned away.

Leila wasn't paying much attention to the exchange between mother and son. She was way too fixated on Alex's pronouncement. "What? Already?"

"Don't let your nerves get the best of you, darlin'. The grand-dame doesn't bite too hard. My last girlfriend only lost two fingers. You have plenty of those to spare," Alex teased as he maneuvered past the wrought-iron gate.

The crush of the stones under the tires acted as a signal, calling to Alex's mother, who appeared on the lower of two side porches. She waved as the vehicle stopped in front of what appeared to be a quaint little carriage house.

"Ready?" Alex asked, primarily of Leila.

She nodded and forced a brave smile.

Alex reached back and squeezed Leila's hand in support, adding a wink before he turned to open the door.

"Hello, Mother. We made it," he called, stretching before reaching for the backdoor handle.

"Alexander, darling, you're here," she answered from her perch overlooking the driveway. She pressed her fingertips against her milky-white cheeks and practically swooned. "Praise be to God, I worried myself silly thinking of that long drive down from Virginia. All those crazy drivers, speeding their way home for the holiday."

Alex started running through the introduction of the Miller family as Leila lingered inside a little longer. *Please let her like me.*

Sara poked her head back in and silently mouthed, "Come on."

Leila inhaled deeply and got out. She nervously stood next to Alex. He put his arm around her waist and pulled her so abruptly to his side that she gasped for breath.

"This, Mother, is the woman who has laid waste to my bachelorhood and enchanted my heart and soul: Miss Leila Angelica Collins, soon to be Mrs. Alexander Ashton Whitfield."

Leila's heart and kneecaps were melting as she absorbed

the intensity of his words and the genuine emotion radiating from his beaming expression. If he wasn't holding her so tightly, she suspected her body would be crumpled in a heap at his feet. She wondered if he anticipated this and planned ahead. The sound of a woman's voice addressing her popped the happy bubble that she easily floated into, leaving her a little behind in the conversation.

"Leila, dear, come up here so I can greet you properly," Constance ordered.

She smiled while Alex pushed her gently toward the house.

Constance met them at the top of the stairs. Elegant taste and refined breeding emanated from her like an expensive French perfume. Although in her early seventies, she looked at least a decade younger. She clearly heeded the warnings about the dangers of sun damage, as her porcelain skin was practically flawless. She was a lean woman standing about five foot six inches tall with a pretty, round face. Her lively blue-gray eyes reminded Leila of a looming storm. She wore a crisp, white, long-sleeved shirt tucked neatly into a pair of tan slacks. A string of graduated pearls hung around her neck. Her thick, silver mane had been gracefully swept up into a bun at the base of her neck, where it was secured by a pearl-encrusted hairpin. Leila was not a woman intimidated by other women, until now.

"Mother." Alex leaned down to give her a peck on the cheek, which she enthusiastically returned.

"Leila, let me give you a big hug," Constance said, stepping forward with outstretched arms.

She awkwardly embraced the older woman. "It's wonderful to meet you. Alex has told me so much about you."

"He has?" she asked. "There really isn't all that much to tell. I'm pretty boring."

"Boring is not a word I would ever use to describe you, Mother," Alex said.

Constance gave him a thankful glance and patted his cheek. "I am simply tickled you could come home for Thanksgiving with Leila and her friends. We have so much to be thankful for, don't we? Bless the Lord, a wedding is on the horizon!"

Alex seemed to take that as a cue to crush Leila against his side for a second time.

"Please come in," Constance said motioning to the door.

Leila felt some of her jitters lift as her future mother-in-law hooked her arm around her left elbow and escorted them inside. She was warm and welcoming and best of all, she seemed sincerely enthusiastic about the pending nuptials.

Jack pushed himself to the front of the group. "Very cool house! Is it haunted?" Jack asked, which prompted an intense and reproachful glare from Sara.

"You never know. This is Charleston, young man," Constance answered, politely.

There better not be any ghosts or Sara will have my head on one of your silver platters. Leila purposefully avoided looking at her after the brief exchange. She was sure her friend's eyes would be burning a hole right through the back of her skull, while silently cursing that she was talked into the trip in the first place. On the other hand, Leila noted that her future mother-in-law didn't look the least bit ruffled. The gracious matron didn't miss a beat in returning to a discussion of their sleeping arrangements.

"Alex, darling, I have you in your old bedroom on the second floor and Leila in the room across the hall. Sara, David, and Jack will be on the third floor with Maxim. His is the last room on the right," Constance explained as they walked through the house. "You may choose among the other rooms."

Leila gasped in delight as she was led through the parlor, into the dining room and to the bottom of the staircase in the grand entrance hall. It was as if she was walking into the early 1800s. Wall-to-wall antiques embellished the magnificent, well-preserved and clearly cherished home. There were seven bedrooms, plus the maid's quarters. The size was clearly geared to a time when families had a large number of children and many servants. The carved moldings, marble mantles, wide plank heart-of-pine floors, oversized original glass windows and high ceilings made Leila reconsider a move.

She was daydreaming of what it would be like to live in such a gorgeous place when she heard Alex ask about the timing of his brother's arrival home. Maxim was a high-end yacht broker. Apparently he was delayed by wrapping up a sale over in Hilton Head.

"I can't wait for you to meet him," Alex said, taking Leila's hand as they ascended the sweeping staircase.

"I can't either," she replied, feeling increasingly relaxed.

About halfway up the stairs, Leila overheard Constance correct Sara. Their hostess explained that she hadn't gone by the name Mrs. Whitfield in quite a number of years. She went by her family name, Ashton. *Makes sense*, Leila thought. She encouraged her own mother to do the same but to no avail. What didn't make sense was that she and Alex were going to have to sleep in separate bedrooms. She decided to bite her tongue since Alex didn't protest the arrangements.

"Pick whichever rooms you want," Alex said to the Millers as they passed by on their way up to the third floor. When the trio was out of sight, he redirected his attention to Leila. "Honey, let me show you where you'll be staying, then I'll run down and get the last of the luggage." He led her to the end of the hallway and opened the door on the left.

The room was bright and cheerful with tasteful, flowered wallpaper. Normally, Leila detested wallpaper, but it seemed to work in this house. A full-sized canopy bed sat facing two long windows that framed the beautiful garden out back. Leila could imagine it in full bloom with azaleas, roses, irises and gardenias. Now in November, most of the plantings were dormant, but not all; camellias were popping open with pretty pink blossoms. She admired the freshly dug beds of purple and yellow pansies that lined the path leading toward a fountain.

Turning away from the window, Leila noticed a small gas fireplace along the side wall. Above it hung an original watercolor of festive day lilies. She read the signature scrawled across the bottom left hand corner. "C-A-P," she said. "Was that painted in the garden?"

Alex came over and stood next to her. "It was."

"The artist has some serious talent."

"Used to," he said. "I'll be right back with your bag. And don't forget to tip the bellman." He winked, then trotted out.

Leila was still standing in the same spot, entranced by the lovely painting, when Sara appeared in the doorway. "Is everything okay upstairs?"

"Fine," Sara answered. "I saw Alex skedaddle and figured I would jump at the chance to see what you thought of Constance. I think she likes you. Good first impression." Sara smiled and gave her friend a thumbs-up.

"She seems nice enough," Leila replied, using a little stepladder to climb up onto the elevated mattress. "She's sure excited about the wedding."

"I bet she's hoping for the pitter-patter of little grand-baby feet next. Someone has to inherit all of this if she wants to keep it in the family. This place reeks of old money. I bet there's some sort of stipulation about that in her will or in a trust. It goes to whoever produces an heir. It could all go to your child."

"Wait a minute! Who said anything about babies?" Leila asked, half-choking on the words.

"Have you talked to Alex about kids? The two of you have ruled that out? I can't imagine you a mother, but then again, I couldn't imagine you a bride either, so as far as I'm concerned, all bets are off," Sara said, resting an arm on the white marble mantel.

"No, we haven't really discussed it. I just assumed that Alex and I were on the same page. Children are out of the question. Diapers, drool, crying – yuck! Plus, I'm thirty-eight and he's in his forties. We would be ancient by the time the brats went off to college!"

Sara smirked. "No, you wouldn't. Having children later in life is in vogue now. You could be like all the other rich working moms and get a nanny."

"Oh, my gosh! Do you think he could want kids?" Leila suddenly felt faint.

"Leila, this is not a conversation to avoid. If you really know for sure that you don't want children, now is the time to discuss it, not the night before the wedding or six months into being married. You can't assume anything. Life expectations change when you get married. He may be harboring a natural assumption that when he finally got married, children would be a part of the picture. A problem arises if the two of you are assuming two different and diametrically opposed things. You won't know that unless you ask," Sara answered.

Leila shook her head in resistance, but Sara's half-smirk and shrug suggested the inevitable.

"Ah, geez. And the first few minutes here went so well. I just knew it was too good to be true," Leila said, collapsing back on the bed.

Sara turned to leave. "Drama queen, don't write things off already. Honestly, could you jump to the worst conclusion any faster? All I'm saying is to find out where Alex stands on the issue. Now get ready. We'll meet you in the *parrrlorrr* in five."

Leila let out an irritated humph. *Well, we won't be having that chat until we get home. The last thing I need is to get trapped here if it goes badly. Isn't having a puppy enough responsibility? Wait! What if that's the real reason he gave me Fifi, to see if I could take care of a dog without killing it? Oh, crud.*

Leila tried to give herself a pep talk as she went into the bathroom to freshen up. She splashed water on her face then stared into the mirror. "I can do this. I'll get through the next few days and then I'll confront it…him. Stay strong. He loves you…me."

Unfortunately, she kept sliding back into an anxiety-filled haze. When she heard the knock on the door, she knew Alex was waiting for her, all happy and loving. "I'll be right out," she yelled, pushing down the knot in her throat.

She ran a brush through her hair, applied a little more color to her cheeks and lips, and forced a smile. When she turned around, he was standing next to the bed staring at her with an odd expression. Two pieces of luggage were on the floor at his feet.

"I told you I would only be another minute," Leila said, feeling irritated over the perceived rush. When he didn't respond, but only blinked, she got the willies. "You okay?"

Alex nodded, then shook his head, as if clearing away cobwebs clinging to his thoughts. "I'm good. How about you? Are you hungry?" he asked, taking her in his arms. "Beatrice, my mother's magician of a cook, prepared a mini-feast."

"Sounds perfect," she lied. The last thing she wanted was

food in her somersaulting gut.

He kissed her softly on the lips, then took her hand. "Shall we?" he asked, snapping back to his usual even-keeled, attentive self.

"Absolutely," she replied, sounding much more confident than she was feeling.

Leila and Alex found Sara, David, Jack and Constance waiting for them in the parlor. Jack was already digging into some small finger sandwiches by the crumbly evidence left around his mouth and the splotch of mustard staining his shirt. It seemed there was never enough food to satisfy the 12-year-old's burgeoning appetite. Sara and David each held a tall glass of iced tea and were being entertained by Constance, who was enthusiastically regaling them with stories from Alex's childhood.

"Are you boring them with my life history, Mother?" he asked, taking a framed black and white picture from her hand. It was a photo shot when he was about 15. He was sitting on the wooden deck of a schooner, his wavy hair blowing in the same direction as the full sails. An 8-year-old, devilish-looking boy was sitting next to him. "I was a dashing young thing, wouldn't you say, Leila?"

"You look like you were posing for a Ralph Lauren ad," she answered.

"Do you still sail?" David asked, taking a sip of the tea.

"If forced to," Alex explained.

Leila listened as her fiancé contrasted his preference for relaxing on the deck of a yacht with a glass of fine wine to Maxim's true passion for all things nautical. She thought it was cute how he bragged about his little brother's skill as a salesman, apparently able to cut deals with everyone from Saudi princes to the little old lady down the street.

"Max has a slick ability to execute his plan with an unyielding single-minded tenacity, all the while showing the utmost discretion for his client's privacy. He does whatever it takes, period. I have to admire that," Alex admitted.

"Sounds a little like a politician," David suggested.

As Leila reached down to pick up a miniature turkey, cheese and avocado sandwich, she perceived an uncomfortable look pass between Alex and Constance, but when she focused, it was gone.

"I can see the similarities," Alex replied, setting the photo down on a walnut console.

"He's a good boy," Constance said, sounding almost defensive. "I'm very proud of what he has accomplished."

"He sounds like he leads a very exciting life," Sara said. "We can't wait to meet him."

Leila finished chewing her food before changing the subject. "Is there anything that we can help with in preparing for tomorrow? Any pies to bake or cranberries to sauce?" She was praying that the answer would be "no" considering that her cooking skills were practically nil.

"Goodness, what a lovely child you are to offer," Constance answered with a refreshed lightness in her voice. "Beatrice has it all under control. She hasn't let us in the kitchen to cook a meal in 20 years, bless her soul."

"Wow, I think Charleston life would fit you to a tee, Leila," David said, flopping down onto the sofa. Leila scowled at him as Sara kicked him in the ankle. "Ow," he mumbled under his breath.

"Mrs. Ashton...," Jack started to say, brushing his shirt with his hand. "Is there a ghost tour that we can go on? I saw a TV program about Charleston not too long ago. You live in a pretty spooky place. But I'm not afraid. My grandmother, Katy, used to be one."

Leila noticed that Sara almost choked on her sandwich as Jack started to explain the supernatural events that took place a few years earlier at their farm. This was only topped by the look of disbelief across Constance's face. Leila had to hold back a laugh.

"Jack, let's not go telling those kind of ghost stories during such a nice visit," Sara suggested strongly enough to make Jack fall quiet. "Sorry. The books kids read these days really excite the imagination."

"Of course," Constance replied, accepting Sara's explanation.

Leila thought that would be the end of it until Alex jumped in. He confirmed that a local company conducted evening ghost tours. When he suggested that Sara accompany Jack on one, Leila knew the answer in advance. *Ha! There's no way she's ever going agree to that one.*

"No thanks. I prefer to avoid stuff like that," Sara replied, glancing at Leila.

"Please," Jack said, his fingers intertwined in full begging mode. "Come on, Mom. Dad and Alex can take me. Right, Dad? When can we go, tonight?"

"Sara, it will be fine," David insisted. "We can take him."

Leila waved her hand dismissively. "Let him go. What's the worst thing that can happen?" In hindsight, she realized that she should have left off the last comment, judging by the stern expression on Sara face. *Oops, stuck my foot in it now. I don't even need telepathy to read her mind; she's about ready to throttle me.*

"You'll have to make reservations," Constance explained, pulling out the local Yellow Pages from a drawer below the bookcase. "I'm not sure they'll have availability tonight. You may have to wait until Friday."

Leila recognized Sara slowly accepting her defeat. A few moments and a phone call later, it was all arranged: reservations for three on Friday night at eight o'clock.

~

Sara was not at all pleased by the prospect of a nighttime ghost walk through the streets of Charleston. She recalled what Ava told her just a few days earlier, that Jack possessed a dormant psychic sensitivity, one that could resurface at any time. *All we need is for him to accidentally attract a spirit, or worse, actually start communicating with the dead.* Sara tried to ignore the prickly feeling tickling the back of her neck, but it only seemed to get more intense.

Flustered, she decided to excuse herself from the small group gathered in the parlor to try to regain her composure. "I'll be right back," she said, setting down her glass of tea.

"Where are you going," Jack asked.

"I forgot to check in with Emma to make sure everything is running smoothly at the farm. I'm going to make a quick phone call," she lied. "I won't be long."

"Wait, I'll come with you," Jack said, getting up. "I forgot my camera upstairs. I want to take some pictures."

Sara would have preferred to be alone, but she couldn't think of a credible excuse quickly enough; Jack was at her side before she blinked. Resigned to having him tag along, she turned and led the way out of the room.

As they were climbing the first flight of stairs, Jack pointed out something unusual. "Hey, Mom, did you notice that there aren't any paintings in the house? Like nada, zero, zip. Kinda freaky if you ask me. Who doesn't hang stuff on their walls?"

Sara glanced around. There were none in the immediate vicinity. "Oh, there has to be. I saw one in the room where Auntie Leila is staying. I'm sure there are others. You just missed them."

Jack shook his head. "Not that I've seen."

Sara had to admit that it was a bit peculiar when they

finally reached the third floor and still hadn't spotted a single frame. *Jack's right, it is weird. Who has a house like this with no artwork? Although just about anything would clash with this busy patterned wallpaper.*

"I'll meet you in your room in a minute," Jack said, sprinting down the hall to his door. "Tell Emma I said 'hi'." Sara had planned on taking Ava's advice by using the brief time alone to breathe deeply and meditate, but now she was too close to getting trapped in her minor fib. She found her cell phone on the dresser and punched in Emma's number. It rang three times before the familiar English accent echoed over the line. Sara sat down on the corner of the bed as she questioned her groom about the status of all the animals. She was saying her goodbyes when Jack appeared in the open doorway and snapped her picture. The sudden flash startled her, making her heart practically skip a beat.

"Jack, please don't do that again. You scared me," Sara scolded, shutting the phone.

"That's what made it so fun. Check out your expression," Jack said, laughing. He handed her the digital camera.

A miniature version of Sara, with her eyes wide and her mouth agape, was frozen on the screen. She scowled at the unflattering image. "Thanks for nothing," she said, handing it back.

Jack looked down at it, still chuckling, but then Sara noticed his joyful expression wane.

"Hey, what's that spot?" he asked, rubbing his finger over the glass. Clearly unsatisfied, he showed it to his mother. "See, it's in the picture. Do you think it's a reflection or that my lens is messed up?"

Sara wasn't sure what he was talking about. "Show me."

He hit a button along the edge of the case and the picture magnified. "Right there."

Hovering to the left side of Sara's head was a white circle. It reminded her of her high school biology class. The thing resembled a human cell, complete with an outer membrane, opaque cytoplasm and a brighter inner nucleus. "It has to be a reflection off the windows," she said. *At least I hope it is, 'cause you're sure to have a fit if your new camera is busted.*

"Yeah, I guess," he muttered, taking it back. "Maybe I should take another without the flash, just to be safe." He stepped back from his mom, bringing her into focus.

"Can I smile this time?" she joked.

"Say 'poltergeist'."

"What?" Sara asked, screwing up her face. Of course, it was at that moment that Jack pressed the button, again trapping her in a less than flattering pose.

He tried to muffle his giggles as he examined what he captured this time around. "It's gone. No dot this time," he said, showing her.

"Good. Now erase those," Sara said, standing up to leave.

"No way, these babies are keepers. You never know when they'll come in handy as bribery material," he replied, trotting out ahead of her and down the stairs.

He used to be such a sweet little boy. Damn hormones. Now all I get is pre-teen sarcasm and blackmail threats.

Sara had just rejoined her family, her host and her friends in the parlor when the sweet sound of cheerful humming ushered a short, round woman in her mid-fifties into the room. She carried an overflowing tray of steamed shrimp.

"Beatrice, good to see you," Alex said, giving her wide girth a hug. "Let me introduce you to everyone."

Sara listened as everyone's name was said as if Alex was reading off an invisible list. When he got to Leila, Sara had to stifle a laugh. The bubbly woman immediately grabbed her friend and smothered her in a tremendous hug. Sara was only half-listening when Beatrice made a comment that was sure to make Leila turn green. "Honey child, God has answered our prayers. You two will make gorgeous babies."

"Auntie Leila, you're having a baby?" Jack asked.

"Jack!" David put a finger to his lips as a sign to be quiet.

Sara was almost certain that Leila was going to land on the floor in a twitching heap, but surprisingly, she made a quick, evasive maneuver. "It's nice to meet you. The food is delicious."

In her mind, Sara heard the same familiar voice saying, "Hell, no!"

"Beatrice, bite your tongue," Constance scolded. "Things must go in the proper order. I would never think of pressuring them."

"Mother, Beatrice, please. This conversation is a little much without a couple of shots of bourbon in me. How about we save this for another time…like never," Alex said.

Sara exchanged an uncomfortable glance with her husband. David tilted his head ever so slightly, a signal for Sara to change the subject, something Leila would be sure to appreciate.

"You know, we would love to walk around Charleston while we still have a little daylight. How about we stretch our legs from our long ride?" Sara asked.

"Yes, of course," Constance said, smoothly gathering her composure after being reprimanded. "Why don't you eat a bit more of the shrimp while it's fresh? I need to run to the kitchen with Beatrice to check on tonight's dinner menu. We'll be sitting down to eat at seven o'clock, so you have plenty of time for a stroll."

Sara watched as the two women made a speedy exit. David and Jack dove right into devouring the food, while

Alex whispered something in Leila's ear.

It wasn't more than 10 minutes before their hostess reappeared. "Have you all finished your snack?" she asked politely, looking over the nearly empty silver tray.

"Yes, Ma'am," Jack replied, enthusiastically.

"Splendid! I've slipped into my walking shoes and I'm ready to show off our sparkling little gem of a city. Charleston is the sultry lady of the South – beautiful, alluring and very steamy."

Sara tousled her son's hair. "We're ready."

"After you, Mother," Alex said, with a gallant sweep of his arm. He held the door open for the parade, taking Leila's hand in his as she passed.

Sara watched as Leila turned to him and smiled.

Out on the sidewalk, the early evening's amber light cast random shadows through the limbs of the massive live oaks.

Sara watched the pattern dance along the ground, making her imagine the path ahead as an enormous and intricate puzzle. She reflexively glanced at the happy couple walking a few strides ahead of her. It was at that moment that Sara remembered how much she hated puzzles as a child. There was always one piece missing, which ended up ruining the whole thing. The distracting spell was broken by the sound of giddy voices ahead. When Sara focused on the present, she realized she was half-a-block away from their small group.

"Sara, what the heck are you doing way back there?" Leila called over her shoulder. "Stop daydreaming and catch up before you get left behind. You're going to miss hearing about the fascinating history and intrigue which unfolded all around us."

David motioned for Sara to join him. She jogged the short distance between them. The return of the jovial chatter and easy laughter between Alex and Leila quickly chased the disquieting visions of an unsolvable puzzle from Sara's restless mind.

CHAPTER SIX

By the end of the first day in Charleston, Leila was mentally and physically exhausted. During dinner, she was able to skillfully dodge the topic of grandchildren, but somehow she faltered when it came to the interrogation about the pending wedding plans. She wasn't certain how it all transpired, but somehow an agreement was forged that they would be married in Charleston on New Year's Eve. Leila could have sworn that Sara's eyes were going to fall right out of their sockets and into her shellfish stew when the wedding date was moved from next spring to a little more than a month away. She was thankful when Constance finally suggested that her visitors retire for the evening. After bidding everyone goodnight, Leila and Alex stole a few private moments together in her room.

"You, my love, made my mother very happy this evening. I'm surprised she isn't on the phone with the caterers already. A new year, a new life. It's going to be perfect," Alex said, gazing down into her eyes with such appreciation and love that it took her breath away.

Leila smiled up at her future husband. "It's going to be ridiculously hectic, but from a practical standpoint, it's the best time for both of us to be away from work," Leila reasoned. "Louie will have everything under control at the vineyard, and it's my slowest time of year at the shop. I usually take some time off anyway; nobody has enough energy after the holidays to redecorate. I envisioned the wedding in Virginia, but if it means that much to you and your mom to have it here, I can be flexible."

"Oh, I know how limber you can be, believe me," he whispered, sweeping her into his arms and kissing her passionately on the lips.

Leila was aroused and seriously tempted to lure him into her bed, but she didn't want to get caught breaking the house rules, at least not this soon. "You better go while I still have a sliver of willpower left," she said.

Alex nodded. He waited patiently while Leila got ready for bed, then dutifully tucked the thick comforter tightly against her waif-like frame and kissed her goodnight. She felt a brief twinge of loneliness when he retreated to his own bedroom, but fatigue was tracking her like a bloodhound after an escaped convict. She readily drifted off under the pleated canopy of the antique bed. Unfortunately, peaceful slumber was a thing of the past and this evening was no exception. The recurring nightmare of being trapped in a bone-chilling, dark place filled Leila's unconscious, making her claw helplessly at the feather pillow under her head. She struggled to break free from the oppressive image. Tiny, terror-filled whimpers escaped from her throat as she writhed under the confines of the crisp, white sheets.

Leila was once again imprisoned by her mind, acutely aware that she was in danger and had to escape. Suddenly a voice filled the space from every direction, lifting her out of her prison. It was a low hungry whisper, tempting and seductive. The sound desperately made her crave its owner, a siren's song that made her ignore her instincts and surrender all will. Leila was at the mercy of her invisible captor. She felt hands caressing her body, lips kissing and licking her neck. Reflexively, she strained toward the warmth, arching with pleasure.

The sound of a fire truck speeding past the house shook her free from the dream's twisted spell. She found herself on her back with the covers off, the lingering sensation of a powerful orgasm still pulsating rhythmically through every muscle. Leila lay still, confused and shivering, as she tried to push away the fog which dulled her senses. She thought she saw the dark outline of a person standing in front of the fireplace. Feeling as if she was coming around from being sedated, she awkwardly squirmed toward the far side of the bed. Fighting off her mounting fear, Leila focused her eyes intently on that one spot, but there was no one else in the room.

"What the…?" she mumbled to herself.

Shaken, Leila slid off the side of the bed and headed toward the bathroom. She flipped on the light and stared at her blood-shot eyes in the mirror. A thin film of sweat coated her naked body, chilling her flushed skin. She felt completely vulnerable and violated, as if she had been lured into a trap. Leila knew her reaction didn't make sense and it was all in her head. Or was it? Feeling completely exposed, she reached for the silk robe hanging on the hook next to the claw-footed tub. The tiny room swirled around her, forcing her to lean on the antique porcelain sink. Leila took a deep breath and twisted open the cold water knob. She filled her cupped hands to the brim with the cool liquid and splashed it across her face. Unfortunately, it didn't quiet her ragged nerves. She quickly dried her damp skin and shut off the light.

The door to the room was unlocked. Leila knew this because Alex kissed her goodnight after she crawled into bed only a few hours earlier. Fending off a growing wave of panic, she took hold of the ornately molded doorknob and searched for a lock. She cursed under her breath when she couldn't find any button to press. "Damn these old things. Where the heck is it?" she asked, as she felt around the edges. All her fiddling caused it to unlatch and inch open.

Leila was about to close it when she spied a man striding down the hallway. A tiny black dog trotted along at his side. The hall sconces were dimmed, cloaking his identity. Leila's first and only instinct was to slam the door shut and hide under the covers, but it was too late. She froze in place.

"Hey there, pretty lady. Hope I didn't frighten you. I'm Maxim," he said walking straight toward her. "I'm surprised to see you up. But then again, this old house has its fair share of rattles and creaks. Brings out a person's primal fears."

Leila was tongue-tied. She simply stared at him blankly.

"You're Leila, right?" he asked. The man's little dog lifted his head, considered her for a moment, then scampered through her legs to investigate the room. "That's Reggie. He sometimes sleeps in there. Not tonight though. Come on, Reg."

Hearing her name was enough to break her trance. "Yes. I'm Leila. Sorry, I'm a little spooked by being in a strange place."

Even through the darkness she could sense that he was running his gaze up and down her barely dressed body. Reflexively, she tightened the belt on her robe and stepped back behind the heavy door.

"I guess I'll see you in the morning. Sweet dreams," he said, turning away and whistling for the old pooch to follow.

The tiny tap-tap-tap from the dog's nails echoed down the hall as he obediently resumed a position at his master's heels.

"Goodnight," Leila replied, taking refuge in her room. She was still leaning against the back of the door when a knock from the other side sent her anxiety to a new height. "Who is it?"

"It's Sara. Let me in."

Flooded with relief, Leila swung the door open, grabbed hold of Sara's arm and brusquely pulled her inside. "God, am I happy to see you! What are you doing down here? And why are you dressed?" Leila asked, giving her a bone-crushing hug.

"I heard you calling me," Sara replied. "I figured something terrible happened."

"What?" Leila asked. "No, I didn't. When was this?"

"I was fast asleep and your voice woke me." Sara replied "I could swear it was echoing up from underneath us, crying out for me. Then I heard a siren, looked out the window to see what was happening and noticed Maxim getting out of his car. It would have been a little awkward meeting him for the first time half-naked wearing only a t-shirt, so I tossed on a pair of jeans."

I can relate. I didn't really anticipate my first encounter with Alex's little brother to be while I was dressed in my robe. But girlfriend, you're hearing things; I never uttered a word.

"Regardless, are you all right?" Sara asked.

"Yes, fine." Leila was already shaken and this conversation wasn't helping her anxiety one bit. "What about David? Did he wake up?"

Leila listened to Sara describe her husband's remarkable ability to sleep through the equivalent of a military bombardment. So ultimately, there was no one to confirm her friend's unlikely account. When Sara began to suggest telepathy as an alternative theory, Leila decided to nip it in the bud.

Leila shook her head. "Listen, I had a pretty freaky dream. The only rational explanation is that I was talking in my sleep."

Sara tilted her head. "I guess that's possible. It must have been a pretty troubling dream."

"If dreams reflect subconscious struggles, I'm not sure what my last one meant. It was disturbing...and erotic. I could have sworn that someone was actually, you know, here with me," Leila whispered.

"Really?" Sara replied. "I suppose that would give me

the heebie-jeebies too."

"I may shatter the fine moral standards of the house, but the only way I'm staying alone in this room tonight is if I'm hog-tied. I'm sneaking over to Alex's bed. I can get back before anyone is up."

"Well, I guess I would worry about you less that way. Just don't let Constance catch you skipping across the hall. She seems pretty old-school, very formal. It would probably kill her."

"Agreed," Leila said, cracking open the door to make sure the coast was clear. "By the way, thanks for checking on me even if it was a false alarm. It's nice to know you have my back."

"Always!" Sara replied.

Leila shut the empty bedroom door and watched as Sara disappeared up the stairs. Silently, she crept into Alex's room, climbed underneath the covers and snuggled up to his warm body without rousing him. She felt safe.

By eight o'clock the next morning, the aromas of the pending Thanksgiving feast filled the air, gently enticing Leila to open her eyes. When she did, she saw Alex sleeping on his side, his arm draped naturally over her ribcage. She was about to carefully lift it so she could slide out and slip back to her room unnoticed, when the door swung open and Maxim bounced in.

"Mornin' A," he called, in a volume way too loud. "Get up."

Leila's reaction was exactly the same as the night before: She froze.

"Uh, wow! Interesting how we meet in the most unusual times and places. What a naughty girl you are, fair Leila," Max said, waving an accusing finger in her direction. "If Mother catches you bedded down with Alexander under her roof, it may very well be roast Leila instead of roast turkey for dinner."

By this time, Alex was stirring, making Leila's stomach do a series of cartwheels and flips. She couldn't bear to face him. She imagined shock and disappointment plastered on his face as he realized he wasn't alone. Compound that with the embarrassment of being caught by his brother and he was sure to cast her out into the street, unworthy to wear the Whitfield name. How did she get herself into this mess? She needed to think, but there was no time; another voice was echoing down the hall. It was a woman with a syrupy-sweet Charleston accent. Leila simply wanted to die.

"Please," she silently mouthed to Maxim.

He gave her a wicked "you owe me" smile and then pulled the bedroom door shut. She hoped he would give her one freebie, but she doubted she would get off that lucky.

"What ?" Alex blurted out, his eyelids retracting as far back as physically possible.

Leila reached forward and covered his mouth with her hand. "Shh, I know I'm not supposed to be here, but your mother is right outside the door," she whispered.

The look she was dreading didn't materialize. Instead, Alex started chuckling under her hand. He peeled it off his face and pulled her to him.

"What a cunning little vixen! Have you been here all night? God, I love you."

"Quiet! She's going to hear you. I don't want her to hate me already."

"Come here," he said, while seductively drawing her closer. "I don't care if she loves you or hates you. All I care about is if I love you…and I do, you wild thing. Why didn't I think of this?"

Leila smiled and kissed him. *What did I do right to get this damn lucky? He is absolutely amazing.*

"Just so you know, Maxim stopped by to say good

morning. Kind of uncomfortable, sorry."

"I'm sure the jealousy is killing him. It's good for him. He thinks he has it all, but baby, he doesn't have you. You're completely mine," Alex said, staring into her eyes.

"I love you so much," Leila replied. Cocking her head to the side, she realized that the house was silent. "Hey, I don't hear them anymore. I'm getting outta here. See you downstairs. I don't want to chance another impromptu wake up call." After one last kiss, she stole away.

CHAPTER SEVEN

By three o'clock in the afternoon, Sara, along with every other guest and member of Alex's family, was obscenely gorged with pineapple glazed ham, turkey smothered in maple-bourbon gravy, cornbread stuffing, mashed potatoes, green beans, homemade applesauce, warm biscuits, and pies of all kinds. Since Beatrice left after cooking to be with her own family, Sara, Leila and Constance cleaned up the remnants of the feast while the men retired to the veranda to smoke cigars. Maxim's little dog, Reggie, followed the women back and forth from the dining room to the kitchen in hopes of salvaging some of the scraps left on the fine china.

That is one funky old dog, Sara thought.

"Reggie, scoot now. You are being a nuisance," Constance ordered, giving the pup a tap with her shoe.

"He's a cute little thing. What kind of dog is he?" Leila asked, scraping food into a little tin that was used for compost.

Cute? Not exactly the term I would use.

"A Schipperke. He's a sailing breed. He turned 22 last summer, an ancient chap. He's gone all gray around his muzzle and can barely see," Constance answered.

"You're joking!" Sara said. "My dogs are lucky if they hit nine or ten."

"They're known for their longevity," Constance explained.

"I don't think he was happy with me last night. I guess I took his bedroom," Leila said.

Sara noticed a sudden and subtle shift in the way Constance was filling the dishwasher. The older woman stiffened for a split second, then relaxed.

"I hope he didn't bother you by scratching at the door.

He's grown accustomed to sleeping in there over the years," she said without straightening.

"I was already up," Leila replied, omitting the rest of the details.

"Was there a problem?" their hostess asked.

Sara detected a hint of coolness in her tone. She thought it might be wise to sway the conversation away from Leila and the previous evening's events. "Gee, Maxim must have gotten him as a teenager. It's hard to imagine having a dog that long. Think of everything he has seen and been through. I remember getting my first dog when I graduated from college and thinking that he would probably be around longer than some of my friends. And it was true. Tragically, a couple of them didn't even live as long as he did," Sara said, pressing down a Tupperware lid on the last of the leftovers.

"Yes, well, looks like we're done," Constance announced, brusquely. "Good work, ladies. Let's find the boys." Without waiting for a reply, she pushed open the door to the dining room and vanished.

Leila and Sara shared a confused look. "What the heck was that about?" Leila asked.

"Not a clue," Sara answered.

"How can talking about the dog get her miffed?"

"Beats me. Just drop it. Everyone has their skeletons."

They took off the aprons they were wearing and joined the group on the porch. Sara was surprised to see that Constance wasn't with them. The two women walked in on Alex telling David what led him into making wine.

"When I left home in my twenties, I was looking to conquer a different world. This is my second career. I retired from my first about 11 years ago. I was an investment banker with one of the big firms on Wall Street. The nineties were very good to me. As I saw it, I could have stayed in that high-octane scene, rich with no life whatsoever, and died from the stress by now, or get out while I was still young enough to explore my other passions."

"No shit! You're so laid back. I never would have guessed." David blurted out, surprised.

"I wouldn't say that," Maxim teased.

Alex shrugged. "Blood pressure of 185 over 120 can really make you reevaluate your life."

"That was a stroke waiting in the wings," Sara said.

Sara sat down on the swing and listened as Alex continued filling the group in on his life story. "My father died from a massive heart attack sitting at his desk in his law office when I was only a baby. I'm not even sure if the memories I have are real or those I picked up from old black and white photographs."

"Alex, you never told me that!" Leila said.

"Now I have," he said, shrugging his shoulders. "It's been a long time. I'm over it. Ralston married my mother when I was a toddler, so to me, he was the one I always called Dad."

"So Max was born after your mom remarried?" Sara asked.

"He was 8 when I came along," Maxim added, puffing on his cigar.

"I'm stunned," Leila announced. "Anything else I should be aware of since I'm marrying into this family?"

"All ancient history, nothing that defines my life or our lives today," Alex answered.

Sara noted a sideways glance that Maxim gave his brother. She wasn't sure how to interpret its meaning.

"You didn't finish telling us how you ended up as a guy in jeans driving a tractor harvesting grapes," Jack chimed in.

Sara was surprised that her son was following the conversation since he appeared to be completely absorbed by his camera. He was sitting next to her, scrolling through all the pictures he had taken since they arrived.

Alex responded to Jack by reaching into the back pocket of his slacks for his worn, leather wallet. He flipped it open, fingered through some business cards and produced a faded photograph. He held it up for everyone to see.

"I loved this old picture of my mom and dad on their honeymoon in Italy. They were pressing grapes with their bare feet. What a hoot! Sure as heck can't do that today, since it's not exactly sanitary. Nonetheless, it stuck in my brain."

Wow, what a strong resemblance between father and son. I wonder if he's more like his real father or his stepdad. Sara took a short leap away from this thought to contemplate how her own attributes were divided. What could be credited to her biological versus adoptive parents?

As a result of the distraction, she missed most of what Alex was saying about going back to school for wine-making and why he didn't want to join the herd in California. Sara assumed that the combination of his business background along with a little common sense kept him on the East coast. There was no arguing that over the last decade Virginia has emerged as a popular and increasingly successful area to grow wine.

"Luckily, money talks; I was able to lure away one of the most well-respected guys in the business to run my vineyard. Louie has been with me since day one. And here I am today, having a great life with a blood pressure of 120 over 78," he said as he plucked the picture back from his fiancé's fingers.

"Lucky for me," Leila said, giving him a kiss on the cheek.

Jack nudged his mother, drawing her attention. "I think my camera is acting up again. That blurry circle is in a bunch of my pictures."

Sara squinted to see what he was pointing at. He was right; it was in at least half of the photos. She considered that it could be a speck of dirt on the lens, but the gray dot seemed to migrate around the screen. "We'll have to bring it in for service when we get home."

He let out an irritated snort and took it out of her hand. Jack had just turned the power off and stuffed it into his pocket when a loud noise from inside the house made everyone turn.

Maxim got up and looked through the window, his expression changed from one of curiosity to worry. "I'll be right back. Mother needs help with something."

"Should I come with you?" Alex asked, starting to follow him to the door.

"No," Max replied, abruptly. "I can handle it. Stay here."

Oh, I hope everything is alright. Constance was acting a little off before.

Sara caught Leila's eye. She could sense her friend was thinking the same thing.

About 10 minutes later, Maxim returned with his mother on his arm. Sara could swear the older woman had been crying.

Alex looked concerned too. "Is there a problem?"

Constance answered evasively. "Silly me, I dropped a box of some old things in the dining room. Thanks to Maxim's speedy assistance, a catastrophe was averted. All is fine."

"Are you sure?" Alex asked, skeptically.

"As I said, everything has been handled by your brother," his mother replied, tightly. There was a barely detectable shift in the older woman's body language, a sudden rigidity.

Sara listened to her answer, but for some reason she didn't believe Constance either. The explanation reminded her of one of those puzzle pieces that had the right shape but just refused to fit correctly, leaving the picture distorted and incomplete.

CHAPTER EIGHT

The dusk ushered in cooler and drier air. The humidity dropped, leaving any lingering moisture to be greedily absorbed by the lush foliage carpeting Charleston. The house was winding down from the day's abundant feast. Constance was the first to excuse herself, apparently suffering from the first pangs of a headache. Sara, David and Jack had their fill of excitement and escaped to their rooms by half past nine. Leila and Alex followed about a half hour later, while Maxim finished a smuggled Cuban cigar out in the garden.

Leila sat cross-legged on her bed with the light on for almost an hour. In spite of the lovely holiday, the descent into darkness forced her anxiety level to rise. The thought of sneaking over to Alex was an appealing option, but she dreaded the possibility of getting caught again.

What should I do? This stinks. She thought about the knowing sideways glances that Maxim had leveled in her direction throughout the day. She couldn't risk a repeat, but her nerves were sizzling, making it impossible to even consider sleeping. Leila rose, pressed her ear against the door and listened for a sign that anyone was still up. Golden silence filled the empty hall.

Okay. A quick brandy or a couple of shots of whiskey and I should be sufficiently sauced and able to pass out. Leila opened the door and quietly padded down the stairs and across the foyer.

Crystal carafes of various liquors were set out in the gentleman's parlor. The room was really a refined study. Leila could picture portly men from past centuries meeting to discuss the politics of the day or the challenges of conducting business in the new world. They would stand around in their tailored suits, sipping scotch while debating the merits of uniting the colonies into their own country, and later, of seceding from the Union. She was lost in this vision when a bright, white streak raced across the far wall. She spun in place, searching for its source. The enormous gas lanterns that blazed brightly outside provided just enough light to bathe the inside of the room in a warm glow. When her eyes adjusted, she spotted Maxim lounging on the sofa, gripping a heavily carved goblet of brown spirits. The light was refracting off the heavy cuts in the glass as he lifted it to his lips. Leila considered leaving, but it was too late. She knew she had been spotted.

"Wandering around in the dark," he said, slightly slurring. "I take it you're still having trouble sleeping? Come on in, join me for a nightcap." He rose and walked over to the decanters.

Leila wished she never ventured down to the parlor this late at night. She thought surely everyone else would be in bed, but she was wrong; now she was stuck having a drink with her intoxicated brother-in-law-to-be. She decided to try to wiggle her way out of the predicament. "Thanks, but no, I really shouldn't. I was actually thinking of some warm milk."

Maxim rotated his torso in her direction, narrowed his eyes and twisted his mouth into a lop-sided grin. "Warm milk? Leila, I think you're shading the truth some. If you were looking for dairy products, what would bring you in the opposite direction, all the way here, to where we house the liquor?"

Leila could feel the cutting sharpness of his gaze, as if he were trying to peel back her protective layer and expose her for who she really was, a coward and a liar. She refused to let him get the upper hand. He had caught her off guard one too many times already. "What strong deductive reasoning you seem to possess. It's true. I was planning on something stronger, but I didn't want to be rude and impose on your solitary enjoyment."

"So what is it then: scotch, bourbon, brandy? What's your pleasure?" he asked, pointing to the selection.

Leila took a couple of steps forward. "What kind of scotch is it?"

"What kind?" he repeated, picking up one of the heavy cut-crystal decanters, "The kind that works this time of night."

"In that case, I guess I'll take it. Is there any ice?"

"Sorry. You'll have to have it neat," he said, shakily pouring the amber liquid into a short tumbler. "Good choice, though. A woman and scotch. I like it. It's a sign of a lady who likes to keep company with the men." He picked up both glasses and went to her side.

Leila took the drink from his outstretched hand. He was standing a little too close. She felt a pang of something: discomfort, fear, attraction, she couldn't quite put her finger on it. She stepped back and took a sip. The strong taste warmed her tense mouth and throat as she swallowed. "Thank you. This should help me sleep." Maxim's unrelenting stare made her feel strangely exposed.

"Nightmares? I've heard that the unconscious can be a merciless guard. It keeps you imprisoned, hopelessly chaining you to your sins and your failings, those unresolved issues that haunt you until you break the cycle and right the wrong," Maxim said, advancing toward her.

"I didn't say anything about nightmares." Leila felt flustered. She didn't appreciate being analyzed. "I'm simply having a hard time falling asleep – strange house, new family, that kind of stuff."

He reached out with his right hand and stroked her flushed cheek with his index finger. "I can see the allure. You are truly beautiful," he remarked, sighing. He leaned closer, the smell of liquor wafting off his breath like a dangerous and hypnotic vapor. "You're simply intoxicating, like a potent drug. You know, the kind you know you shouldn't experiment with, but the temptation is so acute and overpowering that only the strongest can resist. I can only imagine the number of hearts you've left shattered and wasted."

Leila was stunned by his touch and his words. If he wasn't Alex's brother, she was sure he would swoop down and take her in his arms, hungrily kiss her then carry her up the stairs to have his way with her. She was confused and uncertain about what to do next. Was this a test, a real pass, or a drunken moment he would always regret? Regardless, she loved Alex and she wasn't going to play these games with him or any other man. Not anymore.

"Stop it, Maxim," she demanded, backing away. She was hoping that he didn't notice her hands shaking.

The movement seemed to snap him out of it. He smiled a toothy grin, threw back a slug of what she assumed was cognac and went back to the sofa to finish the rest of his drink.

A familiar voice made her turn. Sara was standing in the doorway. "Leila?"

"Sara? What are you doing down here?" Leila asked.

"A party!" Maxim said, slapping his leg. "Would you like a drink too?"

"No, thank you. Leila, could I talk to you privately for a minute in the other room?" Sara asked, beckoning her forward.

"Sure. I was done here anyway. Goodnight, Max, and thanks for the scotch." She was relieved to be escaping the uncomfortable scene.

Leila and Sara walked toward the staircase and stopped.

"What's up?" Leila asked.

"What do you think? I heard you calling me again. I

almost didn't come because I figured you were probably just having another bad dream, but I decided to check on you anyway. You weren't in your room or Alex's, so I came downstairs. I followed the sound of voices and found you and Maxim talking. What were you doing with him?"

"I couldn't sleep. I came to get a drink, but he beat me to it. I think he's pretty lit," Leila answered, avoiding any of the details. "Never mind him. I'm gonna chug this and hope I can sleep the rest of the night." She downed the entire glass in one long gulp, then set the tumbler down on a table in the middle of the foyer.

"Beatrice can clean it up. I'm sure she's used to doing that for Maxim."

"You're killing me with these wake-up calls," Sara muttered.

"I promise I'm not doing anything, so ignore it next time."

"Consider it done," Sara said.

~

Sara wasn't pleased that she was awoken by Leila's psychic echo for the second night in a row. She needed to get control of this accidental eavesdropping. Alex's mother's house was lovely and inviting during the day, but there was something unnerving about it after sunset. Wandering the halls in the dark in search of Leila was a little too spooky for her taste.

Ava told me to meditate and visualize a protective light, but when the heck do I have a free minute to do that? The timing of this trip couldn't have been worse.

Sara checked in on Jack before going back to bed. He was curled up like a pill bug with the covers half over his head. Sara pulled the blanket down enough to give him a soft kiss on the cheek. He looked so peaceful. She imagined him dreaming of dueling knights and swarthy pirates. She continued to be amazed by his resilience; he had easily rebounded, both mentally and physically, after waking up from a coma. He took it all in stride, like it was one more adventure. Sara, on the other hand, found herself even more cautious and overprotective. After her daughter died at birth years ago, she was emotionally devastated. Jack's brush with death, barely a year later, still left her rattled.

"You may look like me, with those sparkling green eyes and brown hair, but boy, are you made of something different," Sara whispered, brushing away a wisp of unruly hair from his forehead. "You are your father's son for sure, coasting through life's ups and downs like they don't even matter. It must be so nice to be free and not a prisoner to silly thoughts of danger. Unfortunately, my nature is to search for artfully crafted half-truths and glimmering false facades. I wish I could inhale some of your trust."

Jack turned over. Sara was about to tiptoe quietly out of the room when she heard a noise outside his window. Curious, she looked down into the garden. Maxim and Reggie were walking down a path toward a stone bench and bubbling fountain. The man staggered a bit, making her wonder if the noise she heard was him bumping into the porch railing or tripping down the back stairs. He stumbled forward the last few steps and collapsed unceremoniously on the bench. Max leaned forward, propped his elbows on his knees and buried his face in his hands. Sara thought he must already be regretting the exchange with Leila. He looked so sad and alone.

Reggie sat obediently next to Maxim's feet for a few minutes then ran off, his curly tail wagging like a pair of hummingbird wings. Sara couldn't see where he disappeared to, but when he returned, he was carrying something thin and about 8 inches long in his mouth. Maxim didn't change his pose at all, seemingly oblivious to the world around him. It was only when the dog dropped his treasure that the man moved. He reached down and picked up what appeared to be a stick. He appeared completely transfixed by the thing for a few minutes. All of a sudden he stood up and started talking to himself, making broad gestures with both arms.

Sara was out of range of hearing what Maxim was saying, but she could tell he was agitated. She tried unsuccessfully to quell her own curiosity; if she couldn't hear what he was ranting about, she at least wanted to know what that crusty old dog retrieved.

Damn, where's a pair of binoculars when you need them! Wait. Jack, you may have exactly what I need.

Sara looked around the room and found his camera. She picked it up with no intention of taking pictures; she was only interested in the 'zoom' feature to get a close up of Max's hand. When it powered on, she magnified the frame to its maximum limit, focusing her eyes on the miniature scene. Sara couldn't be certain, but it appeared to be a paintbrush, not the broad kind that a house painter would use, but the long skinny type an artist prefers. Why this would send the man off into a rambling tirade was a complete mystery. She had seen enough. She pushed the button to shut if off, but the camera snapped a photo instead. Sara gasped, but luckily the flash didn't draw Max's attention. The only one who seemed to notice anything was Reggie. He looked up to the third floor window and cocked his head to the side. *Not bad perception for a half-blind dog.*

Sara was about to turn away when Maxim suddenly noticed the dog's gaze. He followed it straight up to her with piercing eyes. Goosebumps erupted at the base of Sara's neck, spread across her shoulder blades and flowed to every extremity. She suddenly felt very creepy, like a voyeur.

It instantly caused her stomach to roll into somersaults. A jagged pang of guilty anxiety coursed across her nerve endings causing her to accidentally press the button on the camera for a second time. The bright light flashed, making the man outside blink.

Oh, crap! I'm so screwed. How the hell do I explain that?

Sara stepped away from the window. She practically threw the camera back onto the dresser.

The frazzled mother gave her son one more kiss on the top of his head then darted out of the room and back to her own.

CHAPTER NINE

The sound of crows cawing assaulted Sara's sleep. She wasn't sure if the irritating racket was part of a dream or was real. She pried open one droopy eyelid and scanned the thick and gnarly tree branches closest to the window. Half a dozen large, ominous black birds were perched outside, solidifying their angry protest. Apparently, some small, stubborn sparrow dared invade their territory. Sara's mood soured when willing them away didn't appear to have any effect. She hadn't been able to fall asleep until after two a.m., and now these damn birds were pissing her off by relentlessly squawking at the unholy hour of seven.

"Get out of here," she cried. "It's barely even light out." She sacrificed one of her pillows, tossing it aimlessly at the glass to scare them off. Unfortunately, it only made the defiant six-pack turn the volume up another decibel.

Sara was surprised to feel David stir, yawn and then get out of bed.

"Are you getting up?" she asked.

"Yeah, I've been lying awake for about an hour," he answered. "I'm going for a run. Try to sweat off the 10 pounds I piled on yesterday. Why don't you jump start your lazy old bones and come with me?"

"Ugh. Stuff it," Sara replied, pulling the remaining pillow over the back of her head. "Go find someone else to torture."

David changed quickly, smacking her bottom as he departed. "See ya later, Sunshine."

The irritable birds carried on for a few more minutes, then took flight, handing the victory to the small interloper. Sara was finally drifting back to sleep when Jack came barreling into the room at full speed and vaulted onto the empty space on the bed.

"Mom, are you awake?" he asked. He shook her shoulder roughly, as if his raucous entrance wouldn't be enough to raise the dead.

Sara couldn't believe sleep was proving to be so darn elusive. She opened her eyes. "Yup, am now. What's the problem?"

Jack thrust his camera in her face. "This house is haunted. I put this on my dresser last night and when I woke up it was in a different spot; then when I looked at the pictures, there were two I didn't take. It's totally freaky!"

Sara cringed as she recalled inadvertently taking the photos. "No, sweetie, I promise it's not haunted. I took those by accident. When I tucked you in late last night, I noticed Maxim and Reggie outside." She went on to tell him about how being nosey got her into a rather prickly situation. She was incredibly embarrassed over her stint of spying, and worse, Sara was now stuck in the awkward position of having to apologize to Alex's brother. "Take my mishap as an example of why you should always mind your own business."

"But Mom, didn't you see the pictures? Maybe a ghost didn't take them, but it sure looks like you caught one on film."

"Huh?" she uttered. "What are you talking about?"

Jack showed her the digital image captured on the small screen. The first photo showed one of those weird white orbs hovering close to Maxim. Sara dismissed it as a distortion originating from the flash reflecting off the window. Although she did think it was odd that Reggie was starring up at it, as if he could actually see the thing. When Sara scrolled to the second photo, she gasped. *Oh my God!* Maxim was looking straight into the shot and the orb had transformed. The round blob had elongated into what Sara could only describe as a blurry outline of a person. It looked like a smudge, but she could clearly identify the profile of a face, torso and arms. It was impossible to tell if it was male or female. *Holy crap, this can't be.*

Jack must have read the expression of surprise across her face. "See! I knew this place was haunted. It's so cool. All those weird dots mucking up my pictures have to be ghosts. It's like we're on one of those paranormal investigation programs on TV."

Sara sat up in bed. "Jack, I want you to keep this between us. You can't tell anybody."

"Why?" he whined. "I want to show Dad. Plus, if we send it into one of those series we could be famous. Come on, Mom. Don't be such a downer."

Sara bristled at the thought of publicity. The last thing she wanted was to be the one to tell Leila's soon-to-be new family that the living weren't the only ones in residence. In the aftermath of the shock, Leila would make sure she and Jack joined those glowing army of orbs. Downer or not, the information wasn't going any farther than her room.

"It's not an option," Sara warned. "Not a word, young man. This is our secret."

"This sucks!" Jack scowled, snatched his camera out of her hand and stormed out.

Sara didn't have the energy to reprimand him on his attitude or crude language. She was exhausted mentally and physically, but there wasn't any way she was going to get back to sleep after their discovery. *I wonder who it is...was? Maxim was so agitated last night, is it possible he knew a spirit was around? Was he talking to it? Damn, I need a cup of coffee. My brain is too muddled to think about any of this.*

Sara gathered back her disheveled hair into a ponytail, put on a pair of slim brown pants, and a light sweater. Not taking the time to bother with socks, Sara wedged her bare feet into her clogs. She was reaching for the knob when she felt a hard yank on her ponytail, making her head snap back. A bolt of fear sizzled through every muscle of her body. She turned around, only to realize that she was not completely alone. The emotion she felt at that moment was all too familiar; she experienced it a few years earlier when her mother's tortured soul was trapped at their farm.

"Oh, shit. Not again," Sara whispered. She knew what was going on for certain when an angry voice filled her head.

Where do you think you're going? Come back here!

The immediate sensation of being plunged into the center of an ice-cold lake made her reflexively hyperventilate and mentally scramble for solid ground. Sara always assumed that the psychic experiences she endured from the past were isolated events limited by her ties to the McHugh family. It was now painfully clear that she possessed a broader ability to receive messages from the other side, skills she had no idea how to control or, even better, tune out. More than anything, Sara wished she could turn them off at this very moment. *Ava was right again.*

"Please. I want nothing to do with you," Sara explained to no one in particular. "I'm happy to stay out of your way. Go into the light and leave me alone. Really, the light is totally where you want to go." The idea that she could be physically manipulated or harmed by a ghost's concentrated energy was an all too real and terrifying thought. She gathered her courage and took a step toward the door, but froze when she felt something scratch against the side of her neck. A blood-curdling scream echoed in Sara's head, causing her to bring her hands to her ringing ears. She wanted it to stop. The sound seemed to fill every space in and around her.

"What do you want from me?" she asked, not really

wanting to know the answer.

She was startled when the door swung open and the room fell quiet. It was Leila, looking very concerned. "Sara, are you all right?

"Huh?" she uttered.

"I heard you in the hallway," Leila replied. "You sounded really upset, almost panicked."

Sara was incredibly relieved by her friend's presence, but she had to question what she was doing up on the third floor to begin with. *I wonder if she sensed what was happening? Ava thought my emotional state would have to be heightened for Leila to perceive anything and being roughed up by an angry spirit certainly fits the bill.*

"What? You're looking at me funny," Leila said.

"I've had a really bad morning," Sara answered, dodging the truth. "Not enough sleep."

Leila's expression went from confusion to disbelief to something different, something that Sara couldn't quite read. *She knows. She's reading my mind.*

"You're lying," Leila said, taking a step backwards as if she was frightened by Sara. "You're scared. Something has you spooked."

Sara didn't answer. Instead she focused on one word: ghost.

Leila narrowed her eyes at Sara. "A ghost."

She did it!

Leila looked pale. "Please tell me I'm wrong."

Sara wasn't sure whether she should be excited about Leila's breakthrough proving that their telepathic connection flowed both ways, or whether she should be even more rattled. The truth wasn't all that alluring. "I can't."

"Ah geez," Leila moaned. "I don't think I want to know the details. Do you have to tap into a hotline to the wormy and rotting every place you go? Seriously, this is not good."

"Tell me about it," Sara replied. She could still feel lingering goosebumps on her skin.

"So what do we do? Can't you tell it to go away? It's going to mess up my weekend."

Mess up your weekend? I'm the one who had her hair pulled! Sara sure as heck didn't want to stay in the room one more minute. She didn't even want to stay in the house. She wanted to go home, immediately. "Let's make some excuse and leave early. I can say Emma called with an emergency. There's no need to tell anyone the real reason. We can be out of here in a couple of hours, tops."

Now it was Leila's turn to look panicked. "No, we can't. You promised!"

Sara squirmed and felt her neck. She hated breaking a promise, but the situation had changed. She weighed the alternatives. The thought of spending one more minute in that God forsaken room made her insides shiver.

"One night," Leila begged. "That's all I need."

Sara was not happy, but she was having a hard time turning her back on Leila's pleas. "Ugh. Fine. One more night, but if anything else happens, all you'll see is my backside as I high-tail it out of here. Got it?"

Leila nodded. "Understood."

"In the meantime, I might try to dig a little, ask a few pointed questions to see what I can find out about who might have their ethereal knickers in a twist," Sara suggested. "I could use a shield and a bit of ammunition if I get another unwelcome visit."

"No problem, Sherlock," Leila said while opening the door. "I'll stay out of your way."

"Deal. Let's go." Sara knew she was imagining things, but she couldn't shake the feeling she was being watched. Had there been portraits on the walls, she would have expected the eyes to follow her every move. Overnight, the beautiful historic home seemed to wilt away, leaving in its place an empty shell draped in a thick web of melancholy and despair. She nearly catapulted out of her skin when she felt something touch the back of her shoulder. Leila, who was walking next to her, let out a shriek,

"Wow!" Alex said. "I wasn't expecting that reaction."

Sara gasped with relief, but her heart still raced at a sprinter's pace. *Oh, sweet Jesus. This place is going to give me a stroke.*

"For God's sake, don't sneak up on us like that!" Leila snapped.

"Sorry. I didn't think I did," he replied as he gave her a kiss on the cheek. "What has the two of you so jumpy? It looks like you've seen a ghost."

Aren't you perceptive? Sara thought as she made eye contact with Leila.

Alex must have noticed their intense non-verbal communication, because he spoke up. "Ladies? Is there a problem?"

"Your mother's house is haunted," Leila answered bluntly.

She revealed more than Sara would have liked. *Geez, Leila. Forget about subtlety.*

Alex narrowed his eyebrows in what could only be described as a highly skeptical expression. "Seriously, I didn't take you for the theatrical type, at least not in that way."

Leila shook her head. "Actually, it's Sara whose antenna is beeping away. She seems to be a magnet for that kind of thing. I haven't heard or seen anything Halloween-worthy, but relying on past experience, I would take her word for it. You have someone hanging around that hasn't gotten the memo that they died. Personally, I feel pretty blessed that my accident didn't broaden my hearing to include spirits who are bitching about their predicament."

Alex swung his gaze from his fiancé to Sara, who smiled weakly. "What kind of evidence do you have?" he asked.

Damn, I hate this. Why couldn't she have kept her mouth shut so I could have poked around this without making him think that I'm nuts?

"There was a voice…in my head. I couldn't tell if it was a male or female, but it was pretty angry," she explained, nervously playing with her hair.

"I believe you…I do," Alex said. "If you say you heard a ghost, who am I to say you didn't? The truth is that not all of the history in this house is pleasant; some of it has left ugly scars. You can understand. Look at the house you moved into; it had its share of tragedies."

"True." Sara wondered how much he knew about the events that took place on her farm a few years ago. She was going to pry further, but then noticed Alex's eyes grow sad. She stayed silent, shifting her weight uncomfortably from one foot to the other. When he finally looked away, she quietly exhaled. Sara could tell he was debating on whether or not to expose his family's dirty laundry. She waited patiently for him to decide.

"The Ashton family has lived in this house for more than two centuries. During that time a number of people have died here by natural causes, their own hand or another's, so needless to say it's difficult, if not impossible, for me to tell you for certain who you could have encountered. Personally, I know of my grandmother, great-grandfather, and two great-aunts who passed away here," he explained, focusing first on Sara and then Leila. "Life is always complicated. People are fragile, sometimes to a greater extent than can ever be imagined. I know this first hand. My sister, Charlotte, died when she was only a girl."

Sara was shocked by his revelation and fought to find the

right words. "I'm so sorry, Alex, I didn't know. Leila never mentioned your sister."

"Hey, this is news to me too," Leila chimed in.

"I don't talk about her. None of us do…ever. You didn't know because, well, it just never came up. After all these years, I guess silence is a habit."

"But, why?" Sara asked, startled.

"My mother completely broke down. She handled the loss by striking out. In a rage, she told Maxim to burn Charlotte's pictures, her clothes, every trace of her; almost all of it went up in smoke and so did our family. I was lucky. I was gone already, living on my own in New York, so I avoided the worst of the fallout, but it split my parents apart. It was the catalyst for their divorce. Mom couldn't understand my father's reaction. He worked harder and grew more distant, separating himself from the pain. I guess she needed to channel her anger somewhere and Charlotte wasn't here for her to vent against, so the blame fell on my dad's shoulders. My parents couldn't overcome the chasm that developed between them."

"That's terrible," Leila said, gently. "What a tragedy."

Sara couldn't help but think of her own marriage teetering on the brink after her daughter, Grace, was still-born. She didn't like how Alex's story was stirring up agonizing old feelings from her own life. This could have been her and David's ending; they could have divorced and moved to different states to start over. It would have been the easier choice at the time; to avoid having their pain mirrored over and over again in each other's eyes would have been a blessing. Sara was drawn out of her own disturbing memories when she noticed Alex embrace Leila.

"I don't know what to say. My heart aches for your family. It must have been awful for you and your brother," Sara said.

"It was bad. I took it hard, but Maxim was devastated. He was only a kid. He lost his sister and his father, and his mother was a ragged shell of her former self. I typed up my resignation and was about to quit my job to move back home when my father talked me out of it. He insisted that I would be throwing my life away. I was in a skyrocketing career that wasn't going to wait for me to sort out my family problems. He convinced me that calmer waters would arrive once he was gone. And they did. My mother cycled through her grief and made it out the other side. Maxim rose above it and became successful. But to this day, the guilt still gnaws at me. I'm still second guessing the decision to stay in New York."

"It sounds like you made the right decision," Leila said, mustering a supportive voice.

Alex pulled his wallet from his back pocket, opened it and slid out an old photo from a worn fold in the leather.

"That's the three of us. I think that may be the only picture of Charlotte left," he said, handing Leila the faded snapshot.

"She was such a pretty child," Leila said. "I know this is going to sound crazy, but she kind of looks familiar."

"Unless you're lying and you really grew up in South Carolina, I can't imagine how your paths would have crossed," Alex replied. "She's been dead for decades."

"I guess," Leila mumbled, handing the photo to Sara.

Sara carefully took it between her fingers. Captured in the small rectangle were three young faces. She recognized a teenage Alex and much younger Maxim. Between the two boys stood a beautiful young girl about 11 years old with long golden locks, a broad toothy smile and rosy red cheeks that appeared to be artistically painted onto a face as round as a pumpkin. The girl's pale blue eyes sparkled with delight. The captured innocence made Sara feel very sad. She regretted dredging up the past. Surely it wasn't this angelic little girl making threats and yanking her ponytail. She wanted to cry: for Alex, for Charlotte and for her own lost daughter, Grace. She handed the picture back to Alex right before muffled voices started to drift up from down the staircase. Constance was talking to Beatrice in the dining room, but it sounded like she was headed their way.

"If you don't mind, I would prefer that this conversation, you know, about Charlotte and the ghost, stay between us. You can understand how this might upset my mother. She would automatically jump to the conclusion that it was my sister's spirit."

"Of course we won't mention your sister to your mom," Sara said, glancing at Leila who nodded in agreement. "Plus, I'm pretty sure it was a man. This wasn't some little girl going after me; it was someone older, stronger and very determined."

"We don't need to discuss it again, but I'm glad I know," Leila added. "Family secrets have an insidious way of rearing their ugly head in the most unexpected and worst ways. No need to start our life together with something like this stuffed away in your mental attic."

Ain't that the truth? Sara thought. "Speaking of secrets, as far as David is concerned, I have every intention of telling him about the incident in my room and my suspicions. I need him to be aware of the circumstances, but there's no need to share the information about Charlotte."

Alex nodded. "I understand and thanks."

Sara was curious about how Charlotte died, but their meeting was over. Constance was coming up the stairs with an inquisitive expression.

"What are the three of you doing dawdling up here like a band of vagabonds?" the older woman asked, her hands planted impatiently on her hips. "Beatrice has breakfast ready and it's getting cold."

Alex didn't miss a beat. He lied like a professional conman. "We were just talking about how ravenous we are this morning. You're timing is perfect. Are we ready?"

"Bacon and eggs, here we come," Leila answered.

David showed up behind Constance. He was drenched in sweat from his run and was giving off a ripe aroma, even from a distance. Sara muffled a giggle as she watched Constance sniff the air, screw her lips into a sour expression and then step aside, giving David a wide berth.

"We'll meet you in a few minutes," Sara said. "David and I need to discuss something."

"Suit yourself," Leila replied, pulling Alex down the steps.

Once alone, David spoke up. "What's this about?"

"Let's go upstairs and have a little chat, 'cause when you hear it, you're not going to like it," Sara answered, looping a reassuring arm through his. She hadn't planned on telling him or anyone else about the apparition caught on Jack's camera, but the physical manipulation she felt in the bedroom made her reconsider spilling the beans. It wouldn't be wise to keep that kind of experience under wraps. Considering the circumstances, she could use an unwavering ally, and nobody filled those shoes like her husband.

CHAPTER TEN

Leila was picking at the remains of her food, unable to get the image of Alex's poor little sister out of her mind, when Sara and David entered the dining room. She could see by the worried look on David's face that Sara must have told him about her unanticipated run-in with an irritable spirit. As the couple approached the table, Leila shared a fleeting but intense exchange of eye contact with Sara. She didn't need telepathy to know that her best friend's spouse didn't take the news well. There was a peculiar vibe in the room; Leila swore she could feel the tension rise around her like a barrier.

"Please, help yourselves," Constance said. She politely rose from her chair to direct them to the ample buffet set out on the sideboard. "Beatrice has made enough to feed the entire Confederate army."

"I wouldn't be surprised if some of those soldiers were still around," David mumbled, as he started to shovel a small mountain of fluffy eggs onto a plate.

"What was that?" Constance asked, apparently missing the comment.

David turned around, seeming to speak directly to Alex. "Sara and I haven't experienced anything quite like this in a long time. We're a bit overwhelmed."

Alex nodded but didn't reply as David resumed filling his plate.

An uncomfortable moment of silence seemed to suck the oxygen right out of every corner of the room. Leila couldn't take it anymore. "Chow down because we're hitting antique row in 30 minutes sharp. The ladies are destined for King Street this morning. You fellas are on your own. I bet Jack would like to go sight-seeing. What do you think, Sara?"

"The aquarium is supposed to be very nice," Constance said.

"Sure, I guess he would like that," Sara replied half-heartedly.

Leila watched as Sara poured herself a cup of coffee from the ornate sterling service. There was a subtle shake to her hand as she brought the cup of steaming liquid to her lips. It seemed clear that her friend was not at all interested in making small talk, or eating. But that didn't stop their hostess from insisting on both. Leila marveled at Sara's ability not to snap.

The electric sensation of Alex's hand on Leila's thigh popped the mental bubble she had drifted into for a minute. She shivered; it was as if she had been plunged into an ice cold bath.

"Did you hear me?" Alex asked.

Leila shook her head. "No. What? I'm sorry, I wasn't listening. What did you say?"

"I told Maxim that you lovely ladies were going shopping today, so I asked him if he wanted to join us in our sight-seeing extravaganza," he explained as his gaze darted above her head.

"Maxim? Isn't he upstairs?"

The uneasy expression on Sara's face answered her question. Before Leila could react, she felt the man's two hands resting on her shoulders, his musky scent filling her nostrils as he bent down to speak into her ear.

"I'm hurt. You didn't even notice my entrance. I guess you were too busy daydreaming about buying your wedding trousseau."

Leila turned toward his lowered face, their close proximity too uncomfortable to sustain. "Not quite. I'm looking for antiques to pick up for my design firm," Leila replied, while fidgeting in her chair. "Wedding shopping isn't on the agenda for today."

"Come to think of it, while we're out, it wouldn't be a bad idea to explore a few locations for the reception. I'll get straight to work setting up appointments for this afternoon," Constance announced, hustling out of the room so quickly Leila didn't have a chance to respond.

Maxim slid into the empty seat to her right and grinned. "Looks like wedding planning was bumped to the top of the 'to-do' list."

Leila didn't answer. *Super! How the heck did that happen?*

"Max, you never answered me. Are you going to grace us with your company?" Alex asked.

"Sorry, can't do it. I need to run down to Hilton Head for the day. I have some unfinished business that can't wait. I'll be back tonight. Have you ever been out to the island, Leila?"

Hearing her name sucked her back into the moment. "Yes, but it was a long time ago."

"I see," Maxim said. "Did you like it?"

"I guess. I thought it was pretty."

Leila thought back more than twenty years. She had visited the low-key island community with her mother a couple of times after her dad split. She was probably 18 or 19 the last time they rented a cottage. *I have to give her credit. Mom always wanted to vacation there and the jerk wouldn't take her, so when he split, she did it on her own.*

Maxim turned sideways to face Leila as he spoke. "An unforgettable experience, I'm sure. Beach vacations have a way of leaving an indelible imprint."

"Are we going to the beach?" Jack asked, overhearing the last part of the conversation as he joined the rest of the household for breakfast. "Cool!"

Everyone spun around to look at him. He was dressed in

jeans and a long-sleeved, green and blue striped rugby shirt. Jack had combed his wavy hair over to one side, but it was threatening a revolt. As he spoke, his eyes lit up, glimmering with excitement.

Sara shook her head. "You, Dad and Alex are going sight-seeing today."

David smiled in agreement and gave his son a thumbs-up.

"What? That's nuts. Why the heck go look at some old stuff when we can go to the beach?" he asked.

"Jack," Sara replied, sounding irritated by his comment.

"We could do both," Alex suggested. "I haven't been out to Hilton Head in years. We could take a ride, have lunch, kick around in the sand for a bit, then head back and still catch some of the sights around town. One thing I know about my mother is that she'll have the girls in every shop, and now every potential reception site, in the city. I wouldn't be surprised if we beat them back, even with a short side trip. What do you think, Max? Would we get in the way of your business?"

Leila listened quietly as the arrangements were made. Frankly, she was happy to be left out of this excursion. But she had to wonder what kind of mood her shopping partner was going to be sporting. All of Sara's protests were overruled by the guys.

"Seriously, Mom, you need to stop being so overprotective," Jack said, frowning. "It's getting old. I'm not a baby anymore."

David patted his wife on the back. "It will be fine. It seems to be a pretty safe outing. I'll make sure he doesn't dive in with all his clothes on, promise."

"You can give your mother and Leila a complete report when you get back," Maxim told Jack as he pushed his seat back and rose.

Leila watched as he circled around the table and joined Jack at the buffet. Max gave the boy a high-five before heaping a few biscuits into the center of a napkin. He folded the corners up around them, popped a piece of bacon in his mouth and then whistled for Reggie, who came trotting out from under the table.

"I'm going to sail out of here. I need to tidy up my bachelor pad before you hardy chaps arrive," Maxim said, winking at the excited pre-teen.

Leila could tell that Sara was still apprehensive about the day's schedule of activities, but was surprised when her friend unexpectedly bolted from the table to follow Maxim.

"Hmm," David grumbled, as he watched her leave.

"Do you think she's upset about our plans or about…. something else?" Alex asked.

It was clear to Leila that her fiancé was picking up on David's concerned expression.

"Like what?" Jack asked. He sat down in Sara's empty seat with a plate piled obscenely high with bacon and five biscuits.

David's focus moved from Alex, to Jack then to his son's food volume and choices. Leila stifled a laugh as she realized that Jack was completely oblivious to the mixture of awe and disgust he was eliciting from the adults seated around him at the table. It looked like David was about to comment but then abruptly reconsidered.

"Excuse me gentlemen, I'm going to round up Sara so we can start tackling our thrill ride of a day," Leila said. She didn't like the way the morning was playing out and was ready for a change of scenery.

Alex leaned over and gave her a quick kiss. "Have fun, be patient and I'll see you tonight."

Patience, not one of my stronger qualities, Leila thought as she left the room.

~

Sara chased after Maxim, catching him before he climbed into the front seat of his car. With everything that happened since her awakening, she nearly forgot about witnessing his intoxicated rant in the garden the previous evening. When he walked into the dining room, it all rushed back. She felt awkward and uncomfortable around him and knew the only way to alleviate her unease was to address it directly.

"Maxim, wait," she called, jogging the last few strides to his side.

He turned to face the voice preventing him from leaving. Curiosity animated his handsome features. "Yes?"

"I didn't want you to leave without first explaining about last night. I wasn't trying to invade your privacy. I happened to glance out the window when I was leaving Jack's room and saw you were upset. What can I say? The timing appeared suspect, but I swear, it was all very innocent."

Except for that picture of course, but I'm not bringing it up unless you do.

Sara held her breath and waited for his response. The inquisitive expression on his face morphed into one of bewilderment. She could have kicked herself for bringing it up at all. Clearly, he had been too drunk to remember. She should have known better when he didn't act the slightest bit disturbed at the breakfast table. Sara silently berated herself for not picking up on this. She wondered if her collision with the house's irate spirit temporarily threw her radar out of whack. *When will I learn to keep my mouth shut?*

"I have no idea what you're talking about," he said, brusquely.

Sara wanted to cringe as she recognized his reaction devolving into pity, as if she was a lunatic in need of psychiatric care.

Nuts, was the word she thought of. *He thinks I'm nuts. Oh, that's perfect.*

Sara scrambled for something to say, a phrase clever enough to remedy the situation, but before anything coherent came to mind, Maxim gave her a magnanimous pat on the shoulder and dove into his car. He fired up the ignition, put the car in reverse and quickly sped away without a second glance in her direction.

"Ah, shit!" Sara said to herself, kicking at the pearly white pea gravel underfoot. "What a day this is turning out to be. It doesn't pay to be considerate or polite."

Voices riding on the wave of a slight breeze snapped her out of her self-absorption. Leila and Constance were waving from the porch, eager and ready to attack the day. She wanted to scream for the heavens to hear, *What have I done to deserve this?* Instead, she swallowed hard, curved the corners of her mouth into a smile, and forced herself, against her better judgment, toward the house. The hair on the back of her neck bristled as she drew closer. The defensiveness was reflexive, making her picture herself as a cornered and agitated porcupine.

"What were you doing with Maxim?" Leila asked when Sara reached the top step.

"Not important. Let me say good-bye to the boys and I'm ready to go." Not wanting to give either woman any opportunity to pursue it further, Sara walked right past them and through the door. She wasn't about to convey the content of their brief conversation. It appeared as if the explanation was sufficient for Constance, but Leila was like a bloodhound on her heels. When they were out of earshot of anyone else, she felt a hard tug on her elbow.

"Seriously, what was that all about?" Leila asked, under her breath. "You practically tackled the guy in the driveway."

Sara knew that being stuck with Leila for the rest of the day was going to make her life miserable; there wasn't going to be any effective way to dodge the topic.

"Fine, I'll tell you," Sara whispered. "I apologized for sticking my nose where it doesn't belong, but he was too plastered to remember what happened anyway. Satisfied?"

Leila clearly wasn't. She looked more confused than before. "Snooping? When? What did you do?"

"After I rescued you from the parlor last night, I went in to check on Jack." Sara described the entire incident, camera flash and all. "But the weirdest part was his reaction. He was carrying on like a lunatic, but why? Over a paintbrush? What the hell?"

Leila shrugged. "You got me."

Sara could feel her pulse pounding at her temples. "Do me a favor; stay away from him. Family or not, the guy is a bit off-kilter, maybe not certifiable, but definitely therapist-worthy."

"No argument there," Leila replied.

Sara sighed. *Just 20 more hours, not even a full day. I can make it. We can make it.*

"Let's kiss the boys goodbye, grab Constance and go," Sara said. "The sooner we check things off the list, the closer we are to being home."

"After you," Leila replied.

CHAPTER ELEVEN

Leila was as anxious to get out of Charleston as Sara. The arrival of dusk was a welcome sight. After the chaos of the morning, Leila spent the afternoon diverted from the antique shops she had so longingly set her interior designer sights upon. Constance usurped the day, filling it with one appointment after another in search of the perfect reception venue, three-tiered cake, flowers and wedding dress. Leila was on the verge of being one of those "runaway brides" when her future mother-in-law finally called it a day. All Leila knew was that her feet ached, her left hand throbbed and she despised the taste of banana mousse filling.

Sara was a dedicated trouper, standing right by her throughout the ordeal. On several occasions, her friend suggested a quick run to one of those drive-in chapels in Vegas as a cure-all for what was ailing them. Leila initially thought it was a joke, but by the fourth time Sara mentioned it, there was no doubt she meant it. Planning a wedding, even a small one, with only one month until the big day was insane and potentially relationship-ending. Killing the groom's mother was usually a deal-breaker; killing one's self had even greater drawbacks. The only thing that kept her plodding along and biting her tongue was Alex. Love did the impossible: It turned Miss Independent to mush. Six months ago, she would have vividly told Constance where to stuff the bridal bouquet, but now she was dutifully deciding between calla lilies tied with a velvet ribbon or red rose buds gathered together with white satin bunting. The thought of this transformation left Leila unsure about whether she wanted to laugh or cry. Sara was right; eloping might be the only answer.

"We're home!" Constance announced as she maneuvered

her enormous cream-colored, Cadillac into the narrow driveway. "What a productive day. Alex is going to be tickled when he hears how much we've accomplished."

Sara joined in the conversation from where she was sitting in the backseat. "You should consider a late in life career as a party planner. I've never seen anyone so energized and organized."

"Well, that is simply the sweetest thing you could say," she said. "We Southern ladies believe that hosting an event, be it a wedding or charity ball, is a little like creating a piece of beautiful art. It should take everyone's breath away, but the trick is in making it appear effortless. Now let me think, all that is left to do is select the invitations and...."

"And look, the boys beat us home," Leila blurted out, hoping to curtail any further discussion about what still needed to be done.

"I thought they would be back later," Sara said.

Constance swung the front end of the sedan into the spot next to Alex's SUV. "I don't see Maxim's car. He is such a workaholic. I wish he would carve out some time to build a relationship. I don't think he ever bothers to pursue anyone for more than a few dates. Honestly, I don't know what gets in his head. I keep telling him, 'You can't make babies with a boat.' You know the response I get?"

"No," Sara replied, clearly more interested in the conversation than Leila, who flung open her door and was practically leaping from the moving vehicle. "What?"

"That he won't find his soul mate until the books are cleared," Constance answered. "Now for goodness sake, what kind of answer is that? I told him to hire an accountant."

Please, who gives a damn? Leila thought.

"Sounds like good advice. If you wait around for everything to be in order, you will wait forever," Sara said.

Leila left Constance in the driveway to commiserate

with Sara about Maxim's pathetic love life. Frankly, she couldn't care less about the whole topic. Once in the house, she followed the sound of voices to the gentleman's parlor. Alex, David and Jack were lounging on the leather sofas, watching the evening news and snacking on a bowl full of chips. Alex greeted her with a smile as she walked into the room.

"Hey, fellas, did you have a nice day?" Leila asked, stopping in front of the television.

"It would be dramatically improved if I could get a kiss from my lovely wife-to-be," Alex said, curling his index finger as a sign for her to join him.

Leila happily obliged.

"Yuck, kissing is disgusting," Jack declared in a loud bellow as his lips puckered into a sour expression.

"A couple of more years, my man, and you won't be saying that," Alex said, pulling Leila down onto the sofa.

"How true," David added. "So, where is the rest of the wedding planning crew? Did you murder them or give them the slip?"

Leila rolled her eyes. "Neither. They're coming. Sara is doing her best impression of 'Dear Abby.' Sorry, I didn't have the patience to linger. It's been quite a day. My feet are killing me." She slipped her high heels off her aching feet and wiggled her tired toes.

"It's too bad you didn't come with us," Jack said, with excitement. "Hilton Head is so cool. Maxim took us out on one of his boats. It was unbelievably gi-normous! It had a captain and a cook and a bunch of people doing other stuff. We even saw dolphins! Dad thinks we should go back there for a vacation when it's warm."

Leila was amused by his enthusiasm. "That does sound exceptionally cool. Maybe I can go next time."

Alex squeezed his fiancée close. "We'll need to make a

point to visit him next spring."

"I bet Maxim would like that," Jack said. "He is a great guy. You are so lucky that he's gonna be part of your family. We got to go to his house and everything. It's right there on the beach! And you should see the inside. The banister going upstairs looks like the carved lady you would see on the front of old ships and there's a widow's walk, I think that's what it's called, and this stained glass window in the bathroom has a ship crashing into these huge rocks. He said some mythical demon ladies lured the ship to its doom by singing."

"Sirens," David clarified.

"Yeah, that's what he called them. Men fall under a spell."

Jack's description of the house formed a hazy image in the back of Leila's mind. She tried to recall if the cottage where she stayed with her mother years earlier had similar features.

"Hey, kiddo. Who's doing what?" Sara asked, joining the crowd.

"Hi, Mom! Today was a total blast!"

Leila unsuccessfully tried to tune out Jack as he repeated the day's events for his mother's benefit. She snuggled into the crook of Alex's arm, focusing on his scent and warmth. She should have been able to relax, but colors and shapes seemed to coalesce and sharpen as Jack recounted the fascinating treasures he found in Maxim's house. Leila searched for a reasonable explanation as to why the description sounded vaguely familiar. She landed on the notion that these must be typical features in low-country architecture and design.

She shared her opinion when Jack took a breath. "I'm sure all the houses in Hilton Head rely heavily on nautical themes."

Alex shook his head, catching Leila by surprise. "There's no question the island leans that way, but the things that caught Jack's eye are one of a kind," Alex explained. "My dad commissioned the banister to be custom built from a piece of wood salvaged from a colonial ship that sunk off the coast of South Carolina. I've never seen another one like it. And Maxim was the mastermind behind the stained glass window. We gave it to my parents as an anniversary present. Personally, I've always thought it was bad luck, since they were divorced by the next year."

"Oh," was all Leila could muster before Constance entered the room to announce that dinner was ready.

"You boys need to get some nourishment in your bellies. You have to meet the ghost tour in under an hour," she said, leading the way toward the dining room.

A sharp look of concern passed between Leila and Sara at the mere mention of ghosts.

"I think you should cancel," Sara strongly suggested. "It's been a long and ridiculously busy day for everyone, plus we need to be on the road first thing in the morning. It's too much."

"No way, Mom!" Jack replied. "You promised. Come on, Dad. Don't let her ruin our time, please. She's being a chicken."

"Nonsense. Let the boys go have their fun," Constance said, waving her right hand as if brushing aside the whole topic. "The tour only runs for an hour and a half. They'll be home a little after eight o'clock. The child doesn't need that many hours of sleep. Plus, it wouldn't be a real visit to Charleston without an evening trip to the old graveyard. You never know who'll pop up and go *'Boo!'*"

Leila could tell that Sara was going to lose this battle; her whole argument was summarily dismissed as foolish over-protectiveness. Jack was glaring at his mother with his arms tightly crossed over his puffed out chest. David and Alex shrugged their shoulders, clearly trying to avoid getting pulled into the middle of the debate.

"Fine!" Sara said. "Go."

Leila imagined the temperature in the room dipping 20 degrees as Sara spoke. She was thankful when the uncomfortable meal was over and the boys were on their way, but was even more appreciative when Constance excused herself from their company to return an urgent phone message from the president of the local chapter of the Daughters of the American Revolution. After topping off their decaf coffees with shots of Irish whiskey, Sara and Leila escaped to the veranda. The scent of leftover turkey and pumpkin pie wafted along on a mild breeze.

"FYI, this is the last Thanksgiving I'm spending in Charleston," Sara grumbled, blowing the steam across the top of her hot drink.

"Amen to that, sistah," Leila replied, raising her cup in a mock toast. A few minutes of weary silence passed between the two friends. "At least we'll be staying in a hotel when we come down for the wedding. I never thought I would be thankful for some old superstition, but I'm perfectly happy to play along with the one that says the groom can't see the bride before the wedding. It's the perfect excuse for avoiding 'Mommy Dearest' in there."

"She's a lovely lady, the definition of refined with good manners. But holy smoke, it's clear that in this family, it's her way or no way. There is no margin for negotiation, compromise or a difference of opinion; it completely explains why Alex and Maxim aren't married yet. I give you a lot of credit for not bolting. She's going to be a force to be reckoned with, my dear. You better learn how to smile and say 'Yes, Ma'am,' or do yourself a favor and invest in a flak vest and some heavy artillery."

"Thanks, you're tops when it comes to pep talks," Leila said to her grinning friend.

Sara waved her hand as if pointing out a marquee denoting a theatre's current show. "Brash former New Yorker versus dominant Southern belle. It should be quite the match."

Leila smirked. "I can see now why Alex only visits his mother once every year or two. She's positively exhausting."

The two women swayed back and forth on the porch swing in silence while an owl hooted his commentary from a faraway tree branch.

"What do you think they keep in the carriage house?" Sara asked.

Leila contemplated the well-kept little building. *What do most people keep in their garage?* "Junk, yard tools, stuff they refuse to throw away. Why?"

Sara had a curious expression on her face. "Let's check it out. Maybe Constance is a closet hoarder."

"Didn't you already get into trouble on this trip for being a nosy Nellie? Plus, where there are closets there are skeletons. "

"Shut up and come on," Sara mumbled as she rose.

Leila and Sara quietly made their way down the steps and across the pebbled driveway. Through cupped hands, they tried to peek through a clouded window.

"It's too dark in there," Sara whispered. "I can't see anything, can you?"

Leila shook her head. "I say we go in."

Sara nodded. The two women stuck close to the side of the building as they crept around to the entrance.

Leila took hold of the old iron handle and tugged hard. The door didn't budge. She tried a second time with the same result. After shrugging in frustration, she stepped out of the way so her partner in crime could give it a shot. "You try."

Sara planted one foot on the ground and the other against the building for leverage. As she yanked on the handle, a spotlight switched on, illuminating them like a couple of actors on a Broadway stage. It was Maxim's headlights catching them in the act.

"Crap. Now what?" Leila asked.

"Don't act guilty," Sara said, placing her foot back down. "We'll tell him we thought we saw a prowler go into the building."

Maxim switched off the ignition and got out of the car. The stiffness of his movements revealed his displeasure. Reggie poked his head out from behind the man's leg.

Leila felt sick to her stomach, though she wasn't sure why.

Finally, after what seemed like an eternity of making them squirm, Maxim spoke without any hint of emotion. "What are you two doing?"

"What does it look like? We're trying to get the darn thing open," Leila replied, defensively.

"I can see that. The question is, why?"

"We aren't breaking in," Sara answered. "We saw a person slip in there and we were trying to investigate. If anything, we were trying to protect whatever you keep in there."

Maxim cocked his head to one side and lifted his eyebrows in an expression of disbelief. "Really. Is that so?"

"Absolutely!" Leila said in a tough tone. "Why would we lie?"

He side-stepped around the open car door then walked slowly toward the cornered women. The light from the car turned him into a black silhouette. Reggie, a compressed ball of fur, obediently tagged along. Brushing Sara and Leila aside, Maxim reached above their heads to point out a large padlock that was keeping the entry tightly sealed.

"Want to try again?" he asked, smugly.

The shocked expression that crossed Sara's face sent

nervous energy coiling up Leila's spine like a California wildfire fanned by Santa Anna winds.

"Obviously, we were mistaken," Sara said, regaining her composure faster than Leila. "I'm not sure what we saw. The shadows must have been playing tricks on us. Clearly, you've taken precautions against break-ins."

"Clearly." He let go of the silver lock, which fell against the wood with a dull thud.

They watched as he walked back to his car, shut off the lights and hit a button on his key ring, which made the vehicle beep a final comment. Reggie stubbornly lingered at the carriage house, pawing at the entrance. Upon getting no satisfaction, he let out a faint whimper, then chased after his master.

Maxim was set to leave them alone basting in their embarrassment when, on a whim, Leila called out and asked. "What do you keep in there, anyway? It must be pretty valuable."

Maxim's body language spoke volumes as he kept his back to the duo, holding true to his path as he strode away. "Only to me."

After he had disappeared into the house, Leila kicked the door hard enough to leave a dent in the old wood. "What the hell? Has there been some kind of shift in the universe, 'cause I swear this family is giving me the willies. This insanity – the wedding tornado, the angst-riddled brother-in-law, and whatever resident ghosts may or may not be lurking about – was not what I bargained for when I agreed to marry Alex."

"It's going to be okay," Sara said, calmly. "The vibe here is off; we both feel it. So be smart. All of a sudden, you're in a big rush. If Alex is the one, he'll understand if you want to rethink the location or date of the wedding. I'm sure he'll support you. For now, get it together. Make believe you're a blissful and eager bride-to-be…at least until tomorrow."

~

Sara was not thrilled when a frazzled and exhausted Leila decided to turn in before the guys returned from the ghost tour. This left her either alone to fend off grumpy spirits in her guestroom or downstairs to make uncomfortable small talk with Maxim and Constance. It was a difficult choice, but ultimately risking an uninvited exchange with a dead person trumped awkward conversation on the evening's list of acceptable activities. Sara sat cross-legged on the bed and meditated. She focused all her thoughts on creating a protective shield of giant invisible dogs, as well as a cocoon-like force field made up of positive and impenetrable energy. She had achieved a peaceful and relaxed state when a loud noise shattered her calm state. Thankfully, it was only David and Jack, back from their adventure.

"Hey, Mom. What are you doing?" Jack asked as he eyed her pretzel-like position.

"Oh, nothing," Sara replied. "How did things go tonight?"

David rolled his eyes as their son answered.

"It was lame. Yeah, the cemetery was kind of creepy in the dark and so were some of the buildings, but I didn't see any ghosts. Not one!"

"Maybe you were complaining too loudly and you scared them off," David suggested.

Thank goodness. No need to tempt fate.

"You should have gotten our money back. What a rip off," Jack continued, clearly oblivious to his father's sarcasm.

Sara sighed. She felt bad that he was disappointed, but found a degree of comfort in the fact that Jack didn't have his sixth sense primed by the event. David, on the other hand, looked like his last thread of patience was about to snap. Sara braced for the explosion.

"Enough already, Jack," he said. "You were the one who insisted we had to go. What did you expect to see: semi-transparent, floating bodies dragging chains, like something out of an old horror movie?"

Jack squared his shoulders before pulling his camera from his coat pocket. "No, but I at least expected something as good as what Mom caught out in the garden. I got zilch on the tour. Not even one orb!"

Sara could feel the intensity of David's reproachful gaze fall upon her as Jack showed him the photos and explained. *Damn! I guess I should have mentioned those pictures when I told him about the agitated voice and getting my hair pulled this morning. He hates it when he thinks I'm keeping secrets, or worse, getting Jack involved. Like I would want my child to have anything to do with this stuff! How flippin' ridiculous.*

"End of discussion. It's time for bed," David stated coolly.

Sara caught her son's eye before he could protest and shook her head as a warning to throw in the towel or face a battle he would ultimately lose. With a scowl, he quickly gave Sara a kiss on the cheek and turned on his heels to leave.

"Goodnight," David said as Jack left the room.

Sara couldn't make out the pouty boy's grumbled response.

"He isn't even a teenager yet and I want to throttle him," David said when they were alone.

"That's why they start out cute, sweet, and little, so you can fall back on those memories at times like these," Sara suggested, untangling her legs at the same time.

"At least he has raging hormones as an excuse, but what

about you? You somehow failed to mention your surprising new artistic venture."

Sara took a deep breath before answering. After more than 15 years of marriage, she was pretty skilled at verbal acrobatics and was able to diffuse the situation in no time; however there was one point that remained sticky.

"Promise me you'll do everything you can to discourage Jack from pursuing this paranormal stuff," David insisted. "We almost lost him during our first go around, and I'm not willing to play with fire. I didn't anticipate that he would expect the real deal from the tour tonight. I thought he would view it as fun, like the other kids. Who knew he had hard evidence about an actual haunting? Oh wait, you did."

Sara was walking around the room, gesturing with her hands as she spoke. "He only put the pieces together after seeing that one orb all stretched out. I didn't even know there was anything funky on it till he came in to show me this morning. I would have deleted it. I swear. And he has no clue about what happened after he left."

When she stopped to inhale after her long explanation, she absentmindedly glanced out the window. A light shone from the interior of the carriage house. *Someone is in there.* She noted the time on her watch; it was almost 10:40. *And why would that person be out so late at night? What's so important that it requires a padlock to keep it safe?* She was compelled to keep watching to see who would eventually emerge, but David wasn't done with their conversation.

"As long as we're on the same page about Jack, I say we drop it and get to bed," he said.

"I couldn't agree more," Sara responded. The oppressive weight of the day was pressing down on her eyelids, but her curiosity wasn't satisfied. It would never let her drift off to sleep. "Speaking of bed, was anyone else up when you fellas got home? Was Max or Constance awake?"

David shook his head. "Not that I noticed. The house was dark except for the light at the backdoor and those running up the stairs into the upper hallways." He quickly stripped down to his boxers and climbed under the covers. "Get the switch before you get in, okay?"

Sara didn't have much of a choice but to join him. She had already pushed his patience regarding otherworldly phenomena to the edge this evening. Plus, David didn't harbor the same level of mistrust in people and wouldn't understand her irrational desire to sneak away to uncover what mysteries were hidden behind those old wooden doors. She gave the illuminated building one final look and then took her place next to her husband.

CHAPTER TWELVE

After surviving the long holiday weekend in South Carolina, Sara practically got down on her hands and knees to kiss the fertile, Virginia soil. She couldn't wait to get out to the barn and saddle up. Even though dusk was approaching, a short ride across the property was exactly what her brain needed to recover. The trip to Charleston left her deeply worried. The strength of Leila and Alex's commitment was about to be tested; a thorny discussion regarding the pending nuptials awaited the couple at home. If the relationship dissolved under the strain, there was no telling if Leila would ever venture beyond the ingrained pattern of coping she relied on her entire life, one riddled with narcissism and ruled by a heavily barricaded heart.

But her thoughts were plagued by more than Leila's romantic turmoil. Sara's brush with the paranormal during the trip made her seriously contemplate what kept these 'sensitivities' dormant and in check for so long, and more so, what was triggering their seemingly random return. To add one more layer of complexity to the equation, she and Leila were still puzzled by the exchange that occurred with Maxim outside the carriage house. The one thing they agreed on was that her future brother-in-law was highly skilled at broadcasting a slick, carefree playboy veneer to the world. But somehow that evening, the façade had cracked, offering them a glimpse of what was concealed under that polished shell. The cool persona had an icy edge.

Sara slipped out the back door of the house, leaving Jack and David content to catch the remaining quarter of the football game on television. The family's three Great Danes – Madison, Buster, and Sophie – and one Springer Spaniel, Jake, made a split decision on the afternoon activities. The two older Danes chose to stay in the comfort of the house while Sophie, the 11 month-old youngster, and Jake braved the crisp afternoon air in pursuit of a romp through the fields. They zoomed along ahead of Sara, barking a warning to all creatures near and far that an adventure was underway. The rambunctious canines were immediately joined by Emma's two hyperactive Fox Terriers, Bernie and Pippa. As a group, the four-legged balls of endless energy could probably generate enough wattage to power the entire farm.

Sara was pleasantly surprised to see two horses tacked up and ready to go when she entered the barn. Emma was under the flap of a saddle, tightening up the girth on Gale Force.

"Are you joining me?" Sara asked, grabbing her helmet off a hook.

"Wouldn't miss it," Emma replied, popping her bleached blonde head up. "I've been on pins and needles waiting to hear how Leila handled the family introductions. I can't believe she is going through with it."

"Yeah, me too. I'll fill you in as we go. Which ride do you want?"

"Either, it doesn't matter. I can take Edgar," she answered, stepping forward to unclasp the lean, dark-bay horse from his restraints.

"You know, I hate when you call him that. His name is Poe, short for Poetic Justice," Sara said, leading her horse to the end of the barn.

"Be creative. I think Edgar is a more clever play on the literary theme," Emma answered.

Sara shook her head. "Whatever. I'm too worn out to argue."

Sara swung her right leg over Gale Force and gently eased herself onto his strong back. He gave his head an annoyed shake before stepping forward. The swing of his step immediately translated into a soothing effect. *Horses are expensive, but a better use of funds than paying a psychiatrist,* Sara thought.

As they made their way around the perimeter of the property, Sara recounted the events of the last four days. Emma's reaction mirrored Sara's: a cocktail of shock and disbelief topped off by a worrisome dollop of foreboding. Emma was intimately entwined with the last paranormal fiasco. She covered Sara's right flank like a skilled marine when the battle for Jack's life hung in the balance.

"Oh, bloody 'ell," Emma said, her face as pale as Gale Force's coat. "So in addition to reading minds you're conjuring up apparitions?"

Sara nodded. "Sort of, I guess. Bringing Leila back from the other side did something. It created some kind of psychic link between us. We've always been close, but nothing like this. I don't think I'm actually reading her thoughts, but then again, maybe I am. It's totally uncharted territory."

"And the ghost in the room, was it the one in the picture?"

"I have no idea. The photo wasn't all that clear. Plus, I've never actually laid eyes on a ghost. Alex's brother was the only person, dead or alive, I saw in the garden that night."

"Regardless, I hope you left them in Dixie."

"We can only hope."

"What about Jack?" Emma asked. "He picked up on your mum last time. Did he experience anything this time around?"

"Nothing other than figuring out what those orbs were," Sara answered. "They even went on a ghost tour of haunted Charleston last night. He wanted David to get a refund because they didn't see any ghosts."

The Springer, whose nose rarely left the ground, caught the scent of some kind of game and let out his version of a call to hunt. Bernie and Pippa needed no encouragement to charge ahead. Sophie, always eager to lend a hand, bolted straight to their aid. The only problem was that she failed to go around the horses, opting instead for the most direct route by running underneath their bellies. Both horses bristled by prancing and kicking out.

Sara leaned her upper body back to keep her balance while gripping her mount's barrel-like ribcage with her legs. She bit her lip to avoid blurting out a string of expletives.

Emma reached forward with her left hand to stroke Poe's neck while uttering a soothing chorus of "whoas."

The Dane pup and her cohorts were three-quarters of the way back to the barn before the horses quieted down.

"That was good fun," Emma said, sarcastically. "That youngster needs to learn some manners. Darn near tipped me off."

"The exuberance of youth. Bound to leave you injured or dead."

"Ah, back to speaking of the dead. What was David's reaction?"

"If you're asking if he believed me this time, the answer is yes," Sara answered. "Don't get me wrong, he was not the least bit pleased by this resurgence in my, ah…abilities."

"Can you blame 'im?"

"He wanted to leave right away, and in hindsight, maybe we should have, because I'm not at all certain what the future holds for Leila and Alex…or me."

"Do you think she's finally found the excuse she needs to scurry away?" Emma asked. "It wouldn't be the first or even the hundredth time for that matter. Forget interior design; being a well-kept mistress may be her true calling. The woman's practically created a profession out of it."

"Don't remind me," Sara said.

Emma sighed and shook her head. "It'll be a stinkin'

shame if she buggers it up."

"The last few months have literally transformed her. She's broken out of that indifferent, self-serving shell. I'm banking on Alex's patience and strength. He's the lifeline she needs to ward off all the ugliness from the past. She would be lost without him."

"Possibly, or maybe he'll pass her enough rope so she can hang herself," Emma said.

As the sun dropped behind the trees, the horses rounded the final bend on the trail and quickened their pace. They instinctively knew what was approaching – suppertime. The burnt orange and fuchsia sky was fleeting, being pushed farther and lower on the horizon as the darkness spread from the east. On top of the barn's cupola, the last rays of sunshine reflected off the weathervane's bronze arrow. For an instant, it reminded Sara of a lighthouse, warning seafarers that there were treacherous waters to navigate ahead.

She found herself preoccupied by Emma's comments. Alex's family was full of its own complex tragedies, and there was no doubt that each member developed his or her own ways to endure the ebb and flow of life. But Alex seemed fairly unscathed, closer to normal than to certifiable. Sara scoured through her memories of the weekend and all their prior encounters with him, searching for the smallest hint that she missed something underhanded or cloaked about the man who was to marry her best friend. She came up empty. Had Leila found herself the real deal…a decent, honest guy? *I sure hope so*, she thought.

CHAPTER THIRTEEN

In her dream, Leila felt detached, like a spectator watching a sport she didn't understand. There was no fear; there was no emotion at all. She stepped soundlessly through a colorless world. Crisp vapor wrapped around her body like a blanket. What was oddly surprising was that she ceased to breathe yet felt more alive than ever. A dim light sliced a path along the misty ground, guiding her closer to a lone silhouette. Toe to toe, Leila faced the stranger stalking her mind. Like a mirrored reflection, she recognized the dark-haired woman starring back at her. She was looking at herself. Or was she?

A loud mechanical banging shook Leila awake. In a groggy daze, she scanned the immediate area to get her bearings. She was back at the vineyard in Virginia, in Alex's house, and more specifically, in his room. Leila slid her hand through the soft sheets to the place where her fiancé normally slept. It was cold. *But where is he?* The movement roused Fifi, who was snuggled up against Leila's side. The puppy crawled up to Leila's face and licked her nose.

"Good morning, powder-puff. Do you need to go out?" she asked.

The little dog's tail wagged wildly at the suggestion.

The angle of the light streaming through the glass made Leila guess the time was around nine. A colorful rainbow spilled across the wall as imperfections in the original window created a perfect prism.

"I'll take that as a good omen," she said, stretching her arms above her head and yawning.

The sudden cessation of the clamorous noise, which had moments earlier roused her from a fitful slumber, piqued her curiosity. A glance outside provided the answer to Alex's whereabouts. She spotted him near the entrance to the wine cellar. A truck loaded with enormous stainless steel vats was being unloaded.

The sight of the shiny tanks stirred her memory and took her back to the first time they met. Leila had snuck away with her most recent flame, an antiquities dealer named Armistead, for a romantic weekend at a remote bed and breakfast. On a whim, they decided to check out a sampling of the local wineries. As luck would have it, Alex's normal tour guide, Cassandra, was tied up with a family emergency that day. In a pinch, he filled in for her. Somewhere in the mixing room, Leila caught him staring at her with the most impassioned expression. Even now her heart raced as she remembered how Alex zeroed in on her, oozing a kind of alluring, self-assured, masculine charm. By the time they hit the tasting room, she was plotting how to get him alone to slip him her business card. When Armistead excused himself to take an urgent international call, she pounced. Alex's reaction left her shocked. He promptly told her to take her card back. The deflection of her advance stunned her speechless. Then without warning, he leaned forward and kissed her lustily.

Leila reached up and felt her lips. She could almost taste the memory, how then, in a gravely whisper, he sealed the deal. It still echoed through her mind months later, "Fair warning, I don't share…ever. You know where I am when you're ready." He sent her on her way with a friendly wave, as if nothing more had transpired. But something did, and the world shifted underneath her feet. She was bewitched. Leila drove back the following weekend, then the one after that, and the one after that. There was no doubt that this man, this relationship, was very different. He skillfully twisted her life around, making her bend in ways she never envisioned. At times, she was left feeling like a contortionist.

That was the danger she felt during last night's

conversation. When she told Alex about her reservations, she was afraid he would misinterpret them to mean she didn't love him or want to be his wife. The memory of the words she said played over and over in her mind's eye, like a skipping record. "I made a terrible mistake when I agreed to having the wedding in Charleston next month. It doesn't feel right to me. After the last few days, it has morphed into something beyond us, beyond our relationship. I love you and I want our wedding day to be a reflection of that and that alone. I'm so sorry. I know altering our plans will put you in a difficult position with your family, but I don't see any way around it."

He had listened intently, absorbing everything she said about feeling overtaken and rushed. Occasionally, she elicited a nod, but for the most part he remained silent. In the end, he simply got up and left the room; no argument, no opinion, no nothing. That's where it was left, without resolution. Leila fell asleep before he came to bed, and for all she knew, he never did.

Leila was so lost in her thoughts that she didn't notice Alex walking toward the house. It was only when the door cracked open that she snapped back into the present. The smell of his cologne hit her senses before anything else. She turned to find him standing a few feet away. The man could have stepped off a page of an L.L. Bean catalog; he was dressed in jeans, hiking boots, a red flannel shirt, and a fitted barn coat. The two-day growth of stubble on his face lent the finishing touch to the rugged outdoorsman look. Fifi snorted a welcome, dove off the bed and ran through his legs, disappearing down the hall to take care of business.

"You're awake," Alex said, moving closer. "Good. We need to make some decisions."

Leila swallowed hard, fearing the worst. She was about to speak, but he cut her off.

"Right now, this second, what do you want?" he asked. "Do you want to marry me?"

"Yes, absolutely!" Leila answered.

"Then that is what we are going to do. We had a plan, but even the best laid ones change."

"You mean it?" Leila asked, relieved.

"The idea of getting married in Charleston was never mine. It was something spun together by you and my mother. The combination of alcohol, an enchanting location and the desire to go above and beyond to make my mother happy was a powerful combination, but it was never about the two of us and what brought us together. Frankly, I was harboring my own reservations, but you and Mom were so swept away that I bit my tongue and went along with it. I always envisioned the wedding here, at the vineyard."

"You did? Why didn't you tell me that sooner?"

"I didn't get the chance," he replied. "You agreed to Charleston before we had the opportunity to discuss anything. Once my mom heard you would consider a hometown wedding, I knew the vineyard would be a hard sell. The ball was rolling." Alex covered the distance between them and wrapped his arms around her. "I think we were all trying too damn hard."

"How could I have been so blind?" Leila asked. "I thought that was what you wanted. It sounded like a romantic fairy tale, but the more time we were there and plans got underway, the more uneasy I felt. Throw in the creepy stuff with Sara, and I knew it was all wrong."

Alex bent down and kissed her on the lips for a long time. "So let's make it right. Keep the guest list manageable with only close friends and family. No ghosts or ghouls invited."

Leila liked the picture of a small, classy event at the vineyard, one that celebrated who they were together. "Agreed. But when?"

"The sooner the better," Alex said.

"We could stick to the same date, New Year's Eve. What do you think?"

"Perfect," he replied, squeezing her tighter against his chest. "Now, to undo all those other arrangements, I need to make a few calls. Meet me downstairs after you get dressed. I'll be in my office."

Leila noticed the furrows across his brow. "You look worried."

"Nothing for you to be concerned about," he said, releasing her from his embrace. The Westie pup proudly trotted back into the room. Alex glanced suspiciously down the hall. "Nothing other than Fifi droppings on the oriental runner."

"Bad girl! Yuck, I'll clean that up," Leila said. As Alex was closing the door, she shouted, "I love you."

He twisted his head around and winked. "Me, too."

Leila promptly flopped down on the thick comforter covering the bed. It was like falling into a snow drift. All the fears surrounding the wedding evaporated like raindrops from a passing shower. Unadulterated joy beat a steady rhythm through her veins. If she possessed the power to jump through time and land on December thirty-first, she would have charged ahead, leaping enthusiastically. What a difference 12 hours made in her perception of the situation. She spent the next few minutes plotting what needed to be done to pull off the perfect party.

The sound of shattering glass popped her dreamy bubble.

"What the hell?" she shrieked, torpedoing off the bed. Fifi instinctively fled to the far side of the room and barked furiously. On the floor, in the midst of what used to be the window, lay an enormous black crow. Shards of glass littered the wide heart-of-pine planks. The bird's neck was broken and almost severed; scarlet blood trickled steadily from the deep wound. Dislodged on impact and carried by what felt like an arctic breeze, small black feathers floated down like celebratory confetti. The sight of the nearly decapitated bird was gruesome.

"Holy shit! That's not good," Leila said aloud.

The temperature in the room was dropping quickly as 24 degree air rushed inside. Leila quickly threw on some clothes and ran downstairs to find Alex. She could hear him 20 paces away from his office. The tone of his voice froze her in her tracks.

"The plans have changed…accept it."

Leila knew she should go in, but her instincts told her to wait.

"This has nothing to do with Charlotte. Let her rest in peace."

Something smashed against the other side of the wall and fell to the floor. Cautiously, she poked her head around the corner to assess the damage. Pieces of Alex's phone lay scattered about. Across the room, he didn't seem to be fairing much better; he was at his desk, his head bowed. He rubbed his eyes with one hand while pulling at his hair with the other. Obviously, whoever was on the other end of the call didn't take the news well. Leila didn't know whether she should attempt to comfort him or tip-toe away. She lost the option when he suddenly looked up.

"How long have you been standing there?" Alex asked, clearly distraught.

"I…uh," Leila stammered, "…I came to get you. A bird flew through the bedroom window. I didn't mean to overhear. You sounded so upset and angry; I didn't dare interrupt."

Alex turned away, his gaze riveted on the barren vines that covered the landscape. "What did you hear?" he asked, speaking with greater composure.

Leila stepped into the room. "I was able to gather that whoever was on the other end of the line was less than thrilled about our decision to change plans; somehow she, or he, thinks it has to do with your sister. Then you threw the phone. I don't understand. What does she have to do with our wedding?"

Alex wheeled around. Words caught in his throat as he searched for an explanation. "Bringing you to Charleston and including my mother in the planning process was a bad idea. It was a little like raising the dead. Everything got twisted around. It was as if you symbolized everything that was lost. I know it's sick, but through you, it felt like it could be reclaimed."

Leila felt blindsided. "Perfect! Nothing like leaving a good impression. Now what?"

Alex shook his head. "We press forward with our wedding, here at the vineyard, in a month."

"But what about your family…especially your mother?"

He shrugged his shoulders. "It's time to see the past for what it is. Charlotte deserves that much from us. I loved her and I let her down. We all did."

"How?" Leila asked, sitting down in one of the leather armchairs facing his burled walnut desk. "You never told us what happened to her?"

Alex swallowed hard. "Charlotte killed herself. She couldn't live up to my parents' expectations of what a proper Southern lady should be like, act like."

Leila swept her hand over her mouth in horror. The pain in Alex's face tore her heart into ribbons. "I'm so sorry."

"No matter how hard my mother tried to force her, she never fit into the prescribed mold. Every day, it was another lesson: piano, ballet, etiquette, art. They insisted she attend silly cotillions and debutante balls. Finally, Charlotte said 'enough.' She rebelled by chopping off her hair and changing her name. She forced them to see her for who she was; but instead of accepting her, they shipped her off to a psychiatric hospital to be 'fixed.' I intervened and tried to reason with them, to explain that she wasn't crazy, but my words fell on deaf ears." Tears rolled down Alex's cheeks.

Leila went to get up, to wrap him in her arms to soothe the agony, but he stopped her, motioning for her to sit back down.

"No," he said. "I've never had the courage to talk about any of this before. It's about time I let it out."

"I can't imagine the burden of carrying all this around for so long."

"When Charlotte got out, I convinced myself that she would be okay. She spent time at the beach. She seemed at peace, you know, more comfortable in her own skin in spite of everything. My parents thought they succeeded, but the only thing the hospital stay accomplished was to teach my sister how to avoid screwing up when she finally attempted suicide. With one slice of a knife, she cut her carotid artery."

"I don't know what to say. It's so awful, that poor girl. It must have destroyed your family. No wonder your parents split."

Alex nodded, then dropped his head back into his hands. "I never anticipated how finding you, loving you, could complicate things and resurrect the past."

This time, Leila rose and moved around the desk. Hugging him to her chest, she whispered, "You are being way too hard on yourself. No one could have foreseen your sister's death."

"Maybe."

After several minutes of silence, Leila remembered the crow upstairs. The last thing Alex needed at this moment was to clean up a bloody mess, but there was no way around it.

With the threat of snow looming in the forecast, the window would need to be replaced.

"Enough about the past. You're what I need now," Alex said, with a worn smile. "Nobody can rewrite what took place 20 years ago; we can only move forward, and from where I sit, our future is bright and full of promise."

"I couldn't agree more. I hate to tell you this, but the very near future includes a dustpan, a sheet of plywood and nails," Leila said, causing Alex to cock his head to the side as if unable to fully comprehend her last comment. "The window in the bedroom is shattered. A bird flew right through the darn thing. That's the reason I ended up in your office so quickly; I was in dire need of your carpentry skills."

"Perfect, lead the way," he replied, sullenly.

The master bedroom was easily 40 degrees colder than the rest of the house, jump starting the process of rigor mortis; the body of the errant crow had stiffened into a macabre statue. The blood, which drained freely from its neck during Leila's absence, had coagulated into a thick maroon paste. Fifi, adopting a braver demeanor, inched a couple of feet closer and uttered a menacing growl.

"Pleasant," Alex said, poking the corpse with a finger. "It must have hit with wicked force. Quite a determined sucker. A pheasant once came through the dining room window. We always joked about it being an act of protest against eating duck. But a big crow? If I was a superstitious guy, I would be a breaking out the garlic and crucifixes."

Leila arched an eyebrow. *Garlic? What the heck are you talking about?* "You lost me."

"Aren't they supposed to be harbingers of death or evil or something? That's why they're always hanging out with witches in fairy tales and mythology. Hey, come to think of it, what are you doing with one?" Alex asked with a wink.

"You can't blame me; it's your house," she replied.

"I must have skipped those kinds of scary stories as a kid because I just see a poor animal with incredibly defective navigation skills."

"Either way, it's still a mess. Stay put while I find a sack to hold the remains and get the guys to locate the materials to board this up. I'm not sure how quickly we'll be able to get a replacement." Alex gave her a kiss on the cheek, then jogged away.

Leila noticed a jagged piece of glass balancing precariously in the window frame; a brick-colored smudge spread across its edge.

"What possessed you to fly like a kamikaze?" Leila asked. "You should be out in the field, picking at whatever old grapes were left to rot on the ground. Instead you're in here with your head practically cut off."

While considering the lethal injury, Leila squatted down to take a closer look at the bird. Its black eyes stared lifelessly at the ceiling. The sight made her think about Alex's disturbed little sister slitting her own throat. *What on Earth drove you over the edge*? As if trying to rouse an answer from the lifeless animal, Leila reached out to touch it, but instinctively recoiled. A shiver skipped up her spine, suddenly making her very uncomfortable as she waited alone in the room.

"Come here, Fifi. I think we'll let the guys tackle this one on their own." She picked the puppy up in her arms and walked away. *Maybe I'll see if Alex has any garlic in the kitchen, just in case.*

CHAPTER FOURTEEN

As Leila's wedding grew closer on the calendar, Sara found herself growing increasingly anxious, tapping into an irrational fear that disaster was looming. Whether the unspecified catastrophe would come in the form of an all-out meltdown at the wedding ceremony with the bride fleeing like a convict on the run, some shadowy spoiler stepping up to shout "I object" at any given moment, or some other unforeseeable misalignment of the stars was anyone's guess. The only remedy Sara could stitch together was to press on as the consummate cheerleader while telling herself, and anyone within earshot, that all would turn out fine.

In Sara's home, the weeks before Christmas were always a whirlwind fueled by a confectionary overload set to a non-stop choral soundtrack. Cookies were pressed into sugary stars, bells and angels. Presents were wrapped in Santa Claus paper and topped with big red bows. Brave souls fought through desperate crowds to check off that last-minute item on the shopping list. But this year, Sara was strapped with a new slate of items on her agenda: performing her matron-of-honor pre-wedding duties and consulting with an experienced medium for a second time. All these things definitely lacked a "ho-ho-ho" factor.

The first stop on this particular wintery day took her to a one-stop bridal mecca in Falls Church. She picked up the gowns she and Emma would be wearing at the upcoming ceremony, confirmed that the photographer and video crew had the correct directions to the vineyard and talked to the florist about a change in the table arrangements. Leila had dropped most of these last minute details into Sara's overflowing lap. *Oh the joys of being a bridal slave*, Sara thought as she drove to her final destination of the day – Ava

Duprey's office in Old Town Alexandria.

The first time Sara visited the psychic she was surprised to be met at the door without even so much as a knock. When Ava greeted her the second time, it barely registered as unusual.

"Come in, Sara," she said, warmly.

"Happy holidays," Sara replied as she followed Ava into the building.

"Oh, thank you and the same to you. The season is in full swing now, isn't it? But you didn't make the trip here to see me to discuss fruitcake and gingerbread recipes, so tell me, what has you so troubled?"

"These," Sara answered, pulling a stack of pictures from her purse. They were the photos that she and Jack captured in Charleston. She handed them over to Ava, who nodded and started to look through them.

"Ah, orbs," Ava said. "Earth-bound souls, or ghosts if you prefer, are concentrations of energy. When we die our energy is transformed. Electronic devices, such as cameras, video recorders, and radios, can be sensitive enough to pick up the energy that is invisible to the naked eye or ear."

"I didn't realize what they were until I accidentally took the one that produced a partial image of a person," Sara explained. "It's somewhere in the pile."

Ava flipped ahead until she found the print Sara described. She studied it for a few minutes in silence, then closed her eyes as if she was tuning into an internal dialogue.

I wonder if there is a constant stream of dead people conversing in her head. How does she know who is who? And how does she get any rest? Sara was focused on her own thoughts and questions when Ava started to speak.

"It's clear this house has at least one spirit, but it's impossible to tell from the pictures alone. This could be the same orb in each shot or it could be several. The only thing that is clear is that this particular soul was able to use the emotional energy radiating off the person in the photo to create a more sophisticated apparition."

"Do you know who it is?" Sara asked.

Ava shook her head. "I sense a sudden urgency, a need for resolution, but an identity is elusive. From what you told me on the phone, you were in South Carolina with your friend, Leila. She is the one you have the telepathic connection with, correct?"

"Yes."

"Did either of you have any other paranormal situations arise?"

Sara immediately thought of the angry voice yelling at her and her hair being aggressively yanked. The recollection made her shiver. She was anxious to hear Ava's interpretation of the episode. She filled her in on the details and waited for her response.

"Hmm, it is one of two things: Either you encountered a very old and powerful spirit who has been around long enough to be able to interact with our side, or you experienced a phenomenon called place memory. This is where an actual physical location, such as a house or hotel, may harbor the imprinted energy of a tragic event. For those who are sensitive to the other side, the action plays over and over again like a snippet of film reel."

Sara was having a hard time wrapping her head around the idea that an inanimate structure could produce that kind of reaction. *I've bought into a lot of this New Age nutty stuff, but this takes the cake.*

"Think of it as a kind of Post Traumatic Stress Disorder that gets time and place stamped," Ava added. "Individuals who live through the horrors of war or of a violent rape often describe symptoms where they relive the trauma as if it is actually occurring. In a situation like this, if a sudden death or multiple deaths occur, a remnant of the intense energy can be left behind at the location. Mediums who go to visit historic battlefields are prone to seeing a replay of the battle, soldiers fighting with artillery exploding all around."

"That is beyond bizarre," Sara said, shaking her head in utter disbelief.

Ava smiled. "Yes, an accurate description, and chances are you experienced it while you were in Charleston."

"If that's the case, does that mean someone died during a struggle? I was nearly pulled off my feet. Could there have been a murder?" Sara asked, feeling chilled.

"Possibly."

Sara's thoughts zeroed in on Alex's reaction when she and Leila told him what occurred in the guest bedroom. *He said that through the years there were those who died from their own hands or by other's. Maybe one of these circumstances is what I heard and felt.*

"Either way, I wouldn't worry about a ghost following you home," Ava said. "Chances are it is tied to that particular house. But this does reinforce my theory that you are more sensitive to the other side than what you have wanted to believe."

Unfortunately, Sara had to agree with her.

"Have you practiced meditating and surrounding yourself with protective light?" Ava asked.

"Yes, I did exactly as instructed," Sara answered. "I tried to get Leila to do it too, but she isn't quite as willing to get with the program. She gave it a couple of half-hearted attempts and then told me to take a hike. Although she has finally conceded that the telepathy goes in both directions. She can pick up on my thoughts when they're strong."

"Good, that will serve you well in times to come," Ava said.

Sara got a knot in her stomach thinking about Ava's

statement. *What does that mean? In times to come...when is that?* Sara began to open her mouth to ask a question, but Ava cut her off.

"I told you during our last visit that there was movement on the other side, a series of events that have been set in motion to expose a grave error and right a wrong. The first domino was put in place and pushed. The rest will follow. There is a dangerous current ahead that will need to be carefully navigated. You will be asked to use your gifts in ways you never imagined. You will need to trust in your ability to hear what others cannot and then act with conviction. If you don't, someone will die. It is inevitable."

Sara couldn't fathom what she was hearing. *Someone is going to die? What the hell!*

"Be alert, but patient," the medium added.

"For goodness sakes, Ava, tell me what and who is involved so I can do something about it now! Clearly you know what is coming. Why on Earth have me wait?"

"I can't. The specifics are being concealed. It cannot be altered at this stage. I can only see your pivotal role."

Sara felt her heart sink. *This is too much pressure for one person. How am I supposed to know what to do? What if I screw up and someone dies? I can't do it. I refuse.*

"Take this very seriously, Sara. The last domino will fall soon. Be smart and above all, have faith. Your heart will know where the truth lies." Ava handed the pile of pictures back to Sara, then rose from her chair.

Sara was awash in a confused mix of emotions. "Please stop talking in riddles and metaphors. I need hard facts. You're putting me into an impossible situation."

Ava smiled sympathetically. "Dear, it isn't my game, and the other side doesn't play by our rules. You'll find the inner strength when you need it, trust me. All the pieces are being strategically pulled into place. When you stumble across the key, the whole story will emerge."

Sara shivered as her mind pictured a small gold key dangling on a chain, the one that opened her biological mother's diary, revealing the poor woman's most painful and darkest secrets. She wasn't anxious to discover another key, but she realized it was out of her hands. She was being thrust into this role whether she liked it or not. Resigned to her predicament, Sara stood up and walked with Ava to the door.

"I'm a phone call away if you need me," Ava said as she waved goodbye.

Sara nodded but couldn't help but wonder what difference that would make.

CHAPTER FIFTEEN

Leila couldn't believe it was finally here. The morning of the last day of the year was buzzing with activity; a special events catering company arrived on the vineyard grounds at ten o'clock sharp, unleashing a small army of men and women with the assigned task of creating a fairy-tale atmosphere for Leila and Alex's late-afternoon nuptials. The actual ceremony was to be held in the wine cellar; the couple's vows would be recited in front of 40 guests seated between rows of festively decorated French oak barrels. Then it would be time to celebrate.

Tables, chairs, pressed linens, flowers, candles and cutlery were hauled into the reception room over the course of just a few hours. The location was normally used for large group wine tastings and tours, but today it would sparkle with the magic inherent in starting a new life together. Ladders were propped against walls and precariously placed in the center of the floor as thousands of white twinkling lights were strung behind billowy, sheer drapes. The delicate fabric flowed from the middle of the ceiling to the edge of the room and down to the floor, implying that the party was being hosted by a jovial group of angels in heaven. A jazz ensemble, featuring a saxophonist, drummer, bass player, pianist and vocalist, were rolling instruments and sound equipment over to a newly constructed stage. The musicians were in charge of getting everyone up off their cake-inflated tushes to swing the night away on the dance floor.

By noon, Leila's nerves were getting the best of her, making her want to jump in and micromanage the event. It made perfect sense to offer her decorating opinion; taking control was second-nature to her. Historically speaking, it was her *only* nature. She noticed the caterer eyeing a carving-knife when she insisted on changing the seating arrangements for the third time. Luckily, Sara and Emma arrived in the nick of time with a cold bottle of champagne. They whisked her out of harm's way before any blood was shed.

"Bridezilla, what the heck are you doing in there?" Sara asked, leading Leila out of the building and toward the guest house. "They're professionals. They do this every weekend of the year. Leave them alone and come enjoy your day as a bride!"

"You only have a few hours before you're Mrs. Alexander Whitfield," Emma said. "You should be pampering yourself, doing things like taking a soak, sipping outrageously pricey bubbly and handing over your little black book to your single bridesmaid."

Leila smiled. "I knew there was a self-serving reason you agreed to be in the wedding."

"Absolutely," Emma replied with a wink. "I could make a fortune, worthy of any baroness, auctioning that list off on E-bay."

The trio hustled back to the little cottage, popped the cork off the bottle of Moet and giddily toasted the future.

"Here's to a long lifetime of love and happiness for you and Alex," Sara toasted, while clinking her crystal flute against the other raised glasses.

"And to marrying a man with bollocks big enough to keep you entertained and faithful!" Emma cheered.

"Here, here!" Sara added.

"I'll drink to that!" Leila took a long sip, letting the effervescent spray tickle her nose.

Emma choked on her drink and pointed.

Fifi was proudly trotting in from the bedroom dragging an ivory satin pump in her mouth.

"Very bad puppy! No chewing shoes, especially today,"

Sara scolded, chasing after the little white dog. She caught the stubborn Westie's hind legs as she tried to make an escape under the sofa. In a matter of seconds, the damp shoe was pried out of the naughty pooch's jaws.

"Shoot, is it ruined?" Leila asked, holding her breath.

"No, just a wee bit slimy and bent," Sara answered, showing them the damage. "I'll check on its mate and the rest of your things."

"Thanks," the worried bride-to-be replied. "One disaster averted."

"And the weather has cooperated...no rain, no sleet, and no snow. Only clear blue skies," Emma cheerfully reported. "That should count as a good omen. Your guests should be able to motor right over without any trouble."

Please let the day go smoothly. No bad karma allowed within 100 miles of the property. "My brother, Royce, called me from the hotel last night. I still can't believe he decided to fly in from San Francisco." Leila slid onto a stool at the small breakfast counter.

"How long has it been since you've seen him?" Emma asked.

Leila recalled her last trip out to California. It was for a long get-away weekend touring the wineries of the Napa Valley. She and her beau of the moment squeezed in lunch with her brother on their way back to the airport. "It's been years. Four, maybe five."

"It's nice of him to show." Emma put her glass down on the counter. "I didn't see Alex's father at the rehearsal last night either. Is he coming? It would be a bloody crime if he missed it."

"Yeah, and it would be a crime if my dad didn't," Leila said, oozing with sarcasm.

Sara returned from the bedroom. "You need to get over what your dad did. Seriously Lei, it's not healthy for either of you. Take the high road. Remember our lengthy conversation about forgiveness after your brush with death? Life is too short and too precious to hold grudges."

Leila shot her a steely glance. "And you're getting the same response I gave you then. Not a chance, so drop it."

"Fine. It's your day, so consider it done."

"Wise decision," Leila muttered.

Sara quickly changed the subject. "Anyways, Maxim told me his father would be here today. I guess we'll get to finally meet this mystery man."

"He's not that mysterious," Leila explained, finishing off her glass. "He's some big lawyer in Columbia, South Carolina. He moved out there to be closer to Augusta, Georgia and some famous golf course." *It's rather awkward that I won't even meet the man until after I become his daughter-in-law. But on the other hand, that means one less vote on whether or not I'm suitable wife material for Alex.*

Emma was tapping the face of her wristwatch. "God save the Queen, look at the time. If you don't get in the shower now, you're going to be late to your own wedding!"

"Oops. I didn't realize that it was already after three," Leila said, refilling her glass with the delectable French aperitif. "I may need your help zipping up the back of the dress."

"That's what bride slaves are for," Sara replied. "Always at your beck and call, my lady."

Leila smiled like the Cheshire Cat. "Perfect. That's what I like. Unwavering dedication."

"Where should we change?" Emma asked.

"Sorry, there's only one bedroom; you'll need to close the drapes and slip into your gowns out here."

"No problem. Minor inconvenience softened by being closer to the alcohol," Sara replied, shooing Leila away with her hand. "Move it!"

Leila closed the door and took another sip of the sparkling wine. She could still feel the nervous fluttering in her chest, but the palpitations were the result of excitement versus dread. She flipped on the shower and then stood there, carrying on a short conversation in her head as the spray of water warmed up. *Mrs. Alexander Whitfield. Mrs. Leila Whitfield. Sounds good no matter how you say it. Oh geez, I'm really getting married in 90 minutes. Thank God everything is running without a hitch. No ghosts, cranky spirits, or bad juju. That meditation spook repellant stuff Sara made me promise to do this morning apparently works. Now, if I could only picture an umbrella of protective light that would ward off living idiots and assholes, life would be ideal.*

Leila stepped into the steaming shower. The moist heat made her muscles relax in spite of the building excitement. Fifteen minutes later she toweled off, applied her make-up and blew her hair dry. As she was attaching ivory-colored silk stockings to her dangling corset straps, her cell phone rang a chipper song.

"Who the heck is calling me now?" she whined, trying to place the unfamiliar ten-digit number blinking on the ID screen. "Hello?"

"Ms. Collins, this is Jimmy down at the gate. I have a fella who says he's your dad and is here for the wedding, but ma'am, I don't have his name on the list. What do you want me to do?"

Leila froze as if all of her arteries and veins constricted on cue. *It's not possible, he can't be here. He wouldn't be here.*

"Ma'am, are you there?" the man asked. "Did you hear me?"

The heat of Leila's rage melted away the shock. "Yes. I heard you."

"Do I let the guy through?"

"No," she answered. "Detain him. I'll be right down."

"Will do."

Leila spun around, searching for her robe. She could taste decades of anger and resentment on her tongue as she thought about facing her father for the first time in years. *That bastard! How could he do this to me? How could he show up today of all days?*

A voice drifted in from the other room. It was Sara. "Come on, Leila. Time is getting tight."

Leila shoved her feet into her satin pumps, tightened the belt securely around her waist and ripped open the bedroom door. Sara's and Emma's heads nearly knocked together as they twisted to see what was happening.

"What's wrong?" Sara asked. "What are you doing? You're not even dressed."

Leila stormed past the women, grabbed the keys from her purse and snarled a response. "My father is here. Here!"

"Leila, stop!" Sara yelled. "Don't be ridiculous. You can't deal with this now. The ceremony is in less than 45 minutes!"

"Don't you get it? I can't get married without resolving this. He's dropped it on my doorstep, literally."

Leila was outside heading for her car before Sara or Emma could block the exit. Two minutes later, her black BMW sport-coupe skidded to a stop behind the gate house. She bolted out of the vehicle at record speed, almost losing a shoe in the process. Like a soldier on a mission, she marched directly to the entrance of the small building. Before she exploded through the door, an echo bounced along on the frigid December air. Two women in ball gowns were flying down the driveway on a John Deere utility Gator, all the while frantically yelling her name.

"Sorry, girls. Gotta take care of business first," Leila said under her breath.

As she stepped inside, Jimmy took one look at the bride's face and skimpy wardrobe and wisely backed into a far corner. *Clearly, he possesses enough sense to realize that collateral damage is highly possible under the present circumstances,* Leila thought.

Leila scanned the room with the determined precision of a fighter pilot locating the enemy in his sights. Seated against the wall was her intended target. Leila's father was in his early seventies. He was wearing a dark blue pinstriped suit and black wool overcoat.

"Leila, it's been a long time…too long," he said, standing up and taking a couple of steps in her direction.

"Really? That's funny, 'cause I was thinking it hasn't been long enough," she replied. "Why the hell are you here? What do you want from me?"

Emma and Sara burst through the door as soon as Leila began speaking, their hair disheveled and bodies shivering in their forest green, strapless sheaths. Leila glared at them, making it very clear they were not to interfere.

"Royce told me you were getting married today," her father explained, ignoring the intrusion. "I wanted to give you my blessing…and ask for your forgiveness. He told me to stay away, but I couldn't. I needed you to know that I love you and always have."

Leila straightened up and almost laughed. "Love me? You have got to be freaking kidding me! Your blessing? Forgive you? You have 25 friggin' years to apologize and you choose 30 minutes before my wedding? Wow, your selfishness never ceases to amaze me!"

"You're right," he stated, conceding her point. "I should have done this a long time ago. I made a boat-load of bad decisions – choices that hurt you, your brother and your mother. I'm not proud of what I did. I was self-centered. I admit it."

"Let me get this straight. You think you can show up here today, spit out a lame 'I'm sorry and oh, by the way, I love you,' and everything will be fine? The slate will be wiped clean? Hell, maybe you would even like to walk me down the aisle." Leila felt as if every nerve was detonating, building up to a dramatic crescendo, like a fireworks display on the Fourth of July.

The man's eyes desperately pleaded his case. "No, of course not. I only wanted the chance to tell you what was in my heart, and I hope you're happy. I tried calling. I even left messages at your shop before Thanksgiving, but you never called back. I know it will take time for us to rebuild our relationship and for you to forgive me."

At that moment, Maxim opened the door. Sara grabbed his arm and shushed him before he could interrupt.

Leila fought back the sting of tears. "You abandoned us for a girl a few years older than me! Was throwing us away worth it?"

"No," he replied.

"And now you want my forgiveness?"

"More than anything," he begged.

Angry tears ran down Leila's flushed face. "No way. Some things should never be forgiven; like the destruction of a family, betraying your wife and your children. You broke our hearts! We have no 'relationship' and no amount of 'time' is going to fix that. I have no father. He died the day you packed your bags, walked out the front door and never bothered to look back. Do you understand? Now get the hell off this property or I swear to God I'll have Jimmy call the police. Get out!" Leila was trembling from the raw ferocity of her emotions as she pointed a shaking finger to the exit.

"Leila, please. He's trying," Sara interjected, softly.

"Over my dead body," she replied.

The old man bowed his head and did as he was told. "I

really am sorry," he mumbled as he closed the door behind him.

Leila felt completely drained.

"I assume that was your long-lost father," Maxim said.

"Ugly scene…I sure as hell wouldn't want to piss you off. Don't worry about anything, Leila. I'll make sure he leaves."

"Jimmy, if he comes back, shoot him!" Leila ordered, ignoring Maxim.

"Uh…yes, ma'am."

Maxim winked and went to hasten the unwelcome guest's departure.

"Come on, we need to get you back to the cottage and get you dressed," Emma said, gently. "The ceremony is less than 30 minutes away."

Leila straightened her robe and was about to follow her two friends out when she heard Jimmy checking in another guest.

"Hello, Congressman, good to see you again. The ceremony is in the wine cellar."

"Thanks," a deep male voice replied.

Curious, Leila turned to see who he was talking to, but the sedan already rolled away. She was going to ask about the man's identity, but Emma tugged on her to go.

"The guests are going to be waiting," Sara said. "We have to go now."

Leila was too frazzled to protest. "Fine. 'I dos,' here I come."

CHAPTER SIXTEEN

The heated exchange between Leila and her estranged father left Sara with a double knot in her cart-wheeling stomach. After smashing the empty champagne bottle and kicking over a couple of stools, the bride-to-be slammed the bedroom door shut with such force that the entire cottage shook. In the silence that followed, Sara vividly recalled Ava's warning about forgiveness. If the psychic was right, Leila better don a pair of waders instead of a gown because a karma shit-storm was certainly looming large on the horizon. This was no way to start a new life, but any advice would surely fall on deaf ears. Childhood rage has tenacious roots. The wise choice would be to keep all opinions to herself... well, at least until the happy couple returned from their honeymoon. For safety's sake, Sara whispered a silent prayer, begging God's intervention to keep Leila from transferring that boiling animosity to her unwitting groom.

Sara was rummaging around in her purse for an antacid when her best friend re-emerged.

"I'm ready," Leila said, adjusting the sparkling tiara atop her head. The slender woman was a vision to behold. She was dressed in a silk, ivory-colored gown. The form-fitting dress had long sleeves and a scoop neckline that accentuated her shapely assets. Around her throat she wore Alex's Christmas present, a stunning ruby and diamond necklace. A short veil fell to the middle of her back.

"You're positively breathtaking," Sara said.

"Thanks," Leila replied.

"Your fairy godmother already sprinkled the magic dust on the pumpkin and your handsome prince is waiting. Shall we?" Emma asked, waving her hand toward the door.

Leila smiled and nodded.

Sara locked Fifi in her crate, then retrieved their bouquets from the refrigerator. She handed out the compact collection of perfectly opened roses, with the largest spray going into the shaking hands of the nervous bride.

Emma wasn't kidding about the pumpkin. Outside the door, ready to transport the bridal party the mere quarter mile across the property, was a beautiful open carriage drawn by four white horses. The coachman gallantly took each woman's hand as she carefully climbed up the little ladder and was seated on the plush, velvet cushion. Since the ride was so short, the poor fellow was back on the ground and reversing the procedure within minutes.

Sara could hear a string trio playing in the bowels of the wine cellar. The notes of "Ode to Joy" welcomed the anxious women as the gathered crowd waited for the ceremony to begin.

Louie, Alex's groomsman, hustled the last guest down the aisle and dutifully signaled the musicians to change songs. Alex and Maxim were huddled in conversation near the front of the room, but quickly picked up on the cue to take their places.

When the "Wedding March" started, Sara squeezed Leila's arm. "It's time. Are you ready?"

"My feet are still pointed toward Alex, so I guess we can rule out the idea of running off," Leila answered, smiling. "Let's go before some other unforeseen calamity swoops in to muck things up."

"Steel nerves, now, ladies," Emma said before leading their little parade.

"Your turn," Leila said to Sara, breathing deeply.

Sara flipped the veil over her friend's face. "Make sure you're behind me," she whispered, whipping her own bouquet into place.

Halfway up the aisle, she took a quick peek over her

shoulder to make sure Leila was still in the building. Sure enough, her best friend was standing ready at the threshold, looking strikingly beautiful and nervous all at the same time. When Sara reached the makeshift alter, she noticed that Alex's attention was riveted on his bride-to-be. No one word could describe his expression: happy, excited, anxious and proud.

Sara took her place next to Emma and scanned the crowd. David, Jack, and Tom were sitting in the first row with Leila's brother, Royce. On the groom's side, Beatrice sat wedged between Constance and an unfamiliar older man, who, she assumed, was Alex's father. There was an uneven distribution of guests, with a clear deficit on the Collins side. Sara wasn't surprised; the woman was a professional at avoiding emotional tethers of any sort.

The music changed one more time, announcing the arrival of the bride. Leila walked in step to the beat, never taking her eyes off the man she loved. When the last note ended, the bride handed off her bouquet and joined hands with her betrothed.

Sara was impressed by the couple's unflappable composure: no jitters, no tears and most importantly, no sprinting like hell in the opposite direction. She listened as the pastor ran through the standard, "We are gathered here today to witness the joining in marriage of Alexander and Leila... blah, blah, blah." The room remained hushed in reverence to everyone but Sara. An echo rang through the building, bouncing off the walls, a scream of *"No! How could you?"* Sara searched for the source, but found no one. The only trace that something occurred was a sudden rush of cool air and the unmistakable tingling on the back of her neck. By the time the bride and groom recited their vows, Sara was ready to jump out of her skin. She was silently calling on every mental trick Ava suggested. *Protective white light, check.*

Invisible guardians…uh, I hope, check. Concentrating on getting Leila through the ceremony, check-check.

Sara was so absorbed with her own worried thoughts that she was slightly caught off guard when Leila turned to take the ring out of her hand. She snapped back to full attention upon hearing the words, "'The vow I make today will last until the end of our days. With this ring, I forsake all others and pledge my heart and soul to only you,'" flow without a hint of hesitation out of her best friend's mouth. Sara had to admit that it warmed her heart.

The secular ceremony lasted a mere 20 minutes, culminating with a kiss to seal the couple's everlasting bond and Sara uncrossing her fingers and toes.

When the music sprang back to life, the crowd rose to follow the ecstatic couple to the celebratory reception. Leila and Alex stood side-by-side at the wine cellar's exit, thanking each person for attending and accepting their guests' heartfelt well-wishes. Sara was watching the line creep along when Royce walked over to her side.

"Sara," he said, bending his lanky frame over to kiss her on the cheek. "It's been a long time. You're all grown up. David told me you're still a rabid horse fanatic."

She smiled. "You could say that."

"My little sister looks stunning, doesn't she?" he asked, nodding in Leila's direction.

"Like a freshly cut diamond," Sara answered.

"I can still picture her caked in mud and manure from head to toe after you ambushed her at the stable." Royce grinned playfully.

Sara smiled as she recalled the memory. "She held her own. Always does."

"Dad blew his top when he saw the two of you; damn near ruined the car's upholstery."

"Speaking of your dad, did you know he came by about

an hour ago?" Sara asked.

"He called my cell phone. It didn't go well, huh?"

"Not so much," Sara explained. "Your sister constructed her life and identity around your family's collapse. She has a vested interest in hating him. The girl has twisted up her emotions for so long that the very sight of him transported her right back into being a furious adolescent. It was quite a scene. Honestly, I don't think she'll ever forgive him."

"She needs to open her eyes. People screw up all the time."

"You're preaching to the wrong person," Sara said, watching Alex's parents greet their new daughter-in-law. "This is one area that has always been off limits between us; the conversation is over before it begins."

Royce shook his head. "There are no angels on Earth, just regretful ghosts. She should learn this before she becomes one."

Sara bristled at his choice of words. "She has a lifetime to figure that out," she countered coolly as she watched the beaming bride lean down to kiss her mother-in-law on the cheek. Constance hugged Alex, then slid off to the side of the room. Sara couldn't quite interpret the expression on the older woman's face as she lingered, watching the receiving line filter along past the happy couple.

"It is a testament to irony that she married into this family; her new father-in-law is as much of a hound as Dad ever was," Royce said in a low sarcastic whisper.

"How the heck do you know that?" Sara asked, suddenly confused. "Do you know him?"

"I'm surprised you don't. That stodgy old geezer is former Congressman Ralston Powers. He was forced to resign a few years back after getting caught with his pants down while a barely-legal, pretty staffer showed her unwavering support for his cause. Of course, he blamed the girl."

"Get out!" Sara said, giving him a playful push in the shoulder. "We never even heard he was in politics."

"Would you be bragging about him? The guy may be the ultimate archetype for hypocritical Bible-thumper. Do as I say, not as I do."

Sara got an uneasy feeling in her gut as she watched Ralston lean in and give Leila a kiss.

"I knew that S.O.B. from my lobbying days with Equality For All. The man never met a homosexual that he didn't think belonged in treatment or slow-roasting in hell. He's a certifiable homophobe. For the venerable Congressman Powers, equal rights meant equal with an asterisk."

"Don't take this the wrong way, but I see rigidity, stubbornness and bias on both sides of the gay marriage argument. It's a two-way street."

"Not when one side is powerless," he countered with a dismissive wave. "Save your breath; I've heard all the arguments before. But Mr. High-n-Mighty over there, he's one slick character. He came mighty close to talking his way out of his embarrassing predicament, but thankfully, a coalition of preachers stepped in and forced the issue. They had his number. The man is highly selective about what Bible verses the sheep need to follow. Of course, it doesn't apply to him. Picture the slippery ol' dude nailing the Ten Commandments to the courthouse wall, then turning around and using the pages from The New Testament in the can. Not my definition of an upstanding, moral guy."

"I really didn't need that visual," Sara groaned. "Either way, your sister is married to his son, so play nice for the rest of the evening, or else."

"I'll keep my distance. Promise," he replied.

Sara nodded in the direction of the elegant woman dressed to kill in a custom made designer gown. "At least he wasn't married to Constance at the time. No humiliated, loyal-to-a-fault wife to drag in front of the cameras."

"They're not hitched now, but were once," he said with a crooked smile. "All old dogs start out as rambunctious young pups. If he is seducing twenty-somethings in his late seventies, what do you think he was doing at 30, 40 and even 50? Seriously, are you this naïve or do you always view the world through those murky, rainbow-tinted lenses? We can only hope the apple fell far away from the tree."

Sara snorted in indignation. "I'll meet you in the reception room. I need to talk to Leila. Matron-of-honor duties."

Royce shrugged and took off.

Like a spy, Sara watched Leila's eyes follow the old man as he strolled away from the newlyweds and out the door toward the reception. Constance followed closely behind her ex-husband. There was something about the whole scenario that was eating away at Sara's gut. "Damn it! I should have brought along a whole bottle of antacids," Sara muttered under her breath.

When the crowd trickled down to the last well-wisher, Sara swept in to do a little digging.

"We did it!" Leila squealed.

"You sure did," Sara replied, tugging on her friend's arm. "Alex, would you excuse us for a second? I need to ask your wife about a last minute detail. I want the reception to run smoothly, with no unexpected surprises. She'll be back in two minutes."

"You're on the clock. Go," he answered, walking away.

"What is it?" Leila asked. "Did the guard house call? Did my father crash the gate?"

"No, nothing like that," Sara answered, swallowing hard before her next comment. "But I have a question about your father-in-law. I saw the way you looked at him. He was a congressman, your former favorite flavor…."

"So?" Leila replied, a little too evasively.

"Please tell me you didn't, the two of you haven't…met before. Oh, God," Sara said, feeling stomach acid inching its way up her throat.

"What the hell, Sara? I just got married like 10 seconds ago. Do you really think this is the time or place to ask me a question like that? What kind of friend are you?"

Sara thought about this for a moment. She put herself in Leila's shoes and admitted that being pulled away from your husband minutes after saying your vows, only to be interrogated about a relationship with another man, kind of sucked. Unfortunately, Sara's intuition was screaming at her that there was a dangerous undertow ahead. She took a deep breath and plunged in. "The best kind, the kind that is watching your back even if you're not. So, tell me the truth. Is there any history there?"

Leila's icy blue eyes darted away as she snapped her reply. "No. I don't think so."

Sara shook her bouquet of flowers at her friend. "What do you mean by that?"

"Exactly what I said, I'm not sure," Leila whispered. "He's vaguely familiar, but I can't place him. I've mentally checked off all the congressmen, senators and Washington wannabes I've been with in the last 10 years and he isn't one of them. I swear."

"What about beyond that?" Sara asked, pressing Leila to think harder.

"No, I remember the first politician I was ever with and that was 10 years ago," Leila answered. "I was living in Manhattan in the nineties. I dated mostly doctors or businessmen back then, sometimes the occasional lawyer, but certainly not a Southern lawyer."

"Good, that's good. Maybe you caught him on the evening news when he resigned. Your brother told me it was a hell of a scandal. The press must have been all over it."

"I'm not exactly sure what you're talking about, but I guess I could have seen him on television."

"Or it's Maxim," Sara suggested, reaching for an explanation. "You're picking up on the father-son resemblance."

"You think so? I don't see the similarity at all. I think Max looks like his mother."

"Did he act like he recognized you? Imply anything?"

"Nothing," Leila answered, shaking her head. "Believe me, if he was with me, he would have definitely remembered. I leave a lasting impression."

Sara sighed and rolled her eyes. "Humility and modesty are not in your vocabulary, are they?" Leila opened her mouth to answer, but Sara held up her hand. "Stop, I don't care right now. Let's chalk this whole conversation up to a false alarm. The two of you met for the first time 5 minutes ago and no creepy boundaries were ever crossed."

"Right," Leila said.

Sara released a tension-filled breath. "You know what? No good can come from dwelling on this, so I suggest we let it go."

Leila clapped with excitement. "Done. Let's go celebrate."

"One more thing. You didn't happen to hear or see anything unusual during the ceremony?"

"Other than the words 'I do' coming out of my mouth, no, nothing of note. Why?"

"Just checking, Mrs. Whitfield."

When Alex returned, Sara handed Leila to him, then sped ahead to the reception room. She didn't want to interfere with the couple's grand entrance as they were introduced as "husband and wife" for the very first time. As she rushed through the doorway, the toe of her left shoe caught the crinkled edge of the carpet, setting the laws of physics in motion. The momentum sent her body stumbling forward like a drunken cowboy. While trying to avert certain disaster with a passing waiter who was precariously balancing a tray of crystal champagne flutes, Sara tapped into her equestrian reflexes. She instinctively tucked and rolled clear, but her bouquet of flowers did not fair as well. They took an alternate flight path across the room, smashing into the wall.

"Gosh," Sara stammered, straightening up from the impromptu acrobatics. "I'm so sorry."

"Close one," the waiter said, looking a shade or two paler than his ivory-colored uniform. "Champagne?"

"Good idea."

Sara plucked a full glass from his stock before he resumed his duties. After downing half the amount in one quick gulp, she followed the trail of loose rose petals to the sadly dented arrangement. Bending over to pick up the remains of the bouquet, she overheard one side of a heated conversation. It was coming from the far end of the hall. Sara turned around and saw Alex's father sternly giving orders over his cell phone. Clearly, he was not happy. Sara stalled for time by straightening her dress and smoothing her hair. She was close enough to pick up the louder comments he was making to the unfortunate person on the other end of the line.

"I want it done immediately. Do you understand? No mistakes…it has to be clean. Of course I didn't know! If I had, I wouldn't be discussing this now. Alex can't find out the real reason…none of them can. What can I say, Luca? That's why you get the big bucks. You make problems disappear. Now go do your damn job."

Goosebumps spread across Sara's skin like a viral pandemic. She hustled out of range before he turned around. The words could have been about anything: a legal issue, his will, the pre-nuptial agreement. Sara shook her head. *But Leila and Alex didn't have a pre-nup.* Unfortunately, Sara's intuition combined with the Congressman's angry intensity pointed her conclusions in only one direction: toward his son's new bride.

"What now?" she whispered to herself.

Music and cheerful laughter floated through the early evening air, mocking her fears. A voice bellowed over the crowd, asking for everyone's attention. Sara held her breath as she heard the next sentence.

"Everyone, please welcome with a big round of applause, Mr. and Mrs. Alexander Whitfield!"

Sara felt glued to the spot where she stood, listening to the thunderous sound.

Ralston nudged passed her, the scowling rake magically transformed into the joyous patriarch as he strode over to his son's side. Sara suspected that he learned how to turn his charm on and off from years in politics. Watching Leila being twirled around the dance floor by her brand-spanking-new husband, Sara was at a complete loss as to what to do with the information she overheard. The only option was to watch and wait.

CHAPTER SEVENTEEN

Alex lured Leila away from the reception 20 minutes into the New Year. The guests counted down to midnight, toasted to better things to come, then zigzagged their way through the frosty, early-morning air to their waiting cars. Each party was asked in advance to designate a driver to stay sober; otherwise, they were shuttled back to the main house to sleep it off on a stray sofa. Leila would have fallen into the too-tipsy to operate heavy machinery category, but luckily, a warm limousine was idling in the driveway, prepared to whisk them away.

"The luggage is loaded, so off we go," Alex announced, sliding across the rear seat next to his new bride.

"But you haven't told me where we're going," she said, her voice slightly slurred.

"It's a surprise. All I'll say is that you are going to have a trip of a lifetime…something you will never, ever forget."

"Intriguing. How much time do we have until we get there? I was thinking if I can't get you to give in one way, maybe we can close the divider and I can get you to give in another."

"Mrs. Whitfield, you frisky minx," he whispered in her ear. He hit the privacy button on the console as the limousine pulled away from the building.

Oh, Mr. Whitfield, you devil!

Leila awoke from a few short hours of sleep. Excited anticipation of what was to come filled her thoughts as she gazed out the oval airplane window. On the horizon, the blazing, orange crescent was barely visible above the calm, turquoise waters of the Caribbean. The clouds in the expansive sky were being spun by the morning's virgin rays into a beautiful tapestry of violets and pinks as the private jet smoothly touched down on the mountain-lined runway in St. Thomas.

Alex and Leila took a cab a short distance to the port town of Charlotte Amelie, where a 197-foot mega-yacht was docked. With a crew of 10 eager to cater to the newlyweds' every whim, the vessel was ready to set sail. The next leg of the journey would take the couple across the Atlantic Ocean, then into the Mediterranean Sea, with the Italian city of San Remo as their final destination. "Welcome, Mr. and Mrs. Whitfield," an official-looking man said as they reached the main deck. "I'm Captain Van der Hoff."

"Good morning," Alex answered, shaking the man's hand.

"This is for us?" Leila asked suspiciously, trying to take in the enormity of the boat. "No way! We're not really sailing on this!"

"Yes, ma'am," Alex confirmed. "Halfway around the globe."

This is incredible! "I'm speechless. You've truly outdone yourself. I'm the luckiest woman in the world; I found the one man who fully understands the depth of my need to be pampered like royalty."

"Actually, the whole idea was Maxim's," Alex explained, blushing slightly. "He asked me what I was envisioning and before I knew it, he offered this up. He temporarily owns the yacht. Luck has it that it needs to be delivered to the new owner in Italy in two weeks. We get to catch a ride with all the amenities. It's his wedding present."

"It may have been Maxim's suggestion, but you knew me well enough to accept," Leila said, trying to sidestep her previous statement. "Either way, I positively love it!"

"Please, consider yourselves the masters of the ship until we reach our final port," Captain Van der Hoff said.

"Your brother's explicit orders; we can't disappoint now, can we? Luca will show you to your quarters so you can change and get refreshed before we get underway. I'm sure the accommodations will suit you."

A short brunette woman with olive skin and almond-shaped eyes joined their small party. She looked to be in her late twenties. The polite smile on her red lips was stretched a little too tight, making Leila feel like an unexpected inconvenience to the crew's normal routine.

"Luca can give you a tour, detail the scheduled stops along our journey and introduce you to the rest of the crew later this morning," the Captain explained.

"Can we get some breakfast, too?" Leila asked. "I'm famished."

"Of course," Luca answered, with an accent that was difficult to decipher.

"What time will we be embarking?" Alex asked.

"We're waiting for a last minute replacement to our crew," Van der Hoff said, impatiently glancing at his wristwatch. "He should be here within 20 minutes. We'll be pulling anchor shortly thereafter, in approximately 30 minutes."

"Follow me, please," Luca said, leading them into the interior of the ship. "The master suite takes up the front half of the main deck. Your luggage has already been transported to your quarters. If you forgot anything, not to worry. I'm sure you will find the room well-stocked with all the necessities."

By the time they reached their stateroom, Leila was thoroughly impressed. She had sailed on large yachts before, but none approaching this size or level of luxury. The interior was a magnificent example of nautical art deco design. The polished burled woods complemented cream-colored furniture and deep-pile carpet. Rounded edges were offset by sleek, straight lines.

When Luca ushered them into their quarters, Leila drew in a deep breath. It spanned the entire width of the boat.

"I will leave you now," the petite woman stated. "When you're ready, buzz me. Would you like breakfast on the sundeck or the dining room?"

"The deck," Alex answered.

"We won't be long," Leila said. "We want to be outside when we depart."

"Very well," Luca replied, snapping the door shut as she left.

Before Leila knew what was happening, Alex pounced, scooping her into his arms. With two quick steps and a leap, they were sprawled out on the bed.

"I think we have a few minutes to spare," he whispered, growling seductively in her ear.

"This is truly spectacular," Leila uttered before kissing him.

Only a few minutes passed before the sound of the ship's engine starting caught their attention.

"Darn it. The Captain must be getting ready to set sail already. That was quick. It's not even close to being a half-an-hour. Do you want to go on deck and have a toast?" Alex asked.

"Absolutely!" Leila replied. "Give me a minute or two in the bathroom to freshen up." She retrieved the smallest of her bags. It held her cosmetics and other vital essentials.

The bathroom was a spectacle to see with polished marble, platinum fixtures, an enormous soaking tub and an oversized shower with body jets shooting in from multiple angles.

Leila gazed into the mirror; her face seemed to glow with happiness. She unlatched the top of the hard, leather travel case, then riffled through it, plucking out what she needed. After reapplying her make-up, brushing her teeth and combing her hair, she had only one more detail to take care of. With all the excitement surrounding the day of the wedding, she forgot to take her birth control pill. Leila's heart skipped a beat when she realized the little plastic packet was missing. In a stomach-churning flash, she remembered setting it out in the guest cottage next to the bathroom sink. She usually swallowed the tiny pink tablet at bedtime but planned on popping one before the start of the ceremony so she wouldn't forget. There the darn thing still sat. *Some good that did me! Now what?*

The ship's engine grew louder and the ship lurched ever so slightly, marking their departure.

"Come on, Leila," Alex called. "We're going to miss chugging out of the harbor."

"Um, Honey…?" she said, cracking open the door. "We have a problem."

Alex squinted at her skeptically. "What?"

"I forgot my pills. We have to tell the Captain to stop. You need to go to a drugstore to buy a bunch of condoms."

Alex chuckled. "You want me to tell Van der Hoff to turn the boat around so I can get a box of rubbers? You're insane."

"This is serious," Leila said with a huff. "The last thing we want is for me to get pregnant."

Alex pulled her to him. "I know that wasn't our plan, but would it really be that awful? I can imagine a mini-version of you wrapping me around her little pinky."

Leila felt her throat close up. She was almost too stunned to speak, but after forcing herself to breathe, she answered. "Damn right it's not the plan, you said so yourself. You told me having a baby wasn't a sticking point to our relationship… our marriage."

"And it's not, but if it happened, it would be okay. I love you, and I would love our child. Even an unplanned one."

She struggled to break free of his embrace. "No, no, it wouldn't! I don't want a baby!"

Alex sighed and glanced out the window. The moment went from blissful happiness to... something else. Something Leila felt but couldn't quite put a name to.

"Fine," Alex said, shrugging. "Why don't you check the drawers? Luca said they stock the thing with toiletries. Maybe they have a stash of condoms."

Leila spun around, feeling stung and misled. She went back to the bathroom and opened the cabinets but found nothing. She was starting to panic when Alex called her name.

"I found some. There's a fresh box in the nightstand. Catastrophe averted, so let's enjoy the rest of the trip."

Leila was relieved, but was uneasy about their uncomfortable exchange. She wanted to clarify their positions and come to a final consensus, but a knock on the door prevented her from speaking.

A voice on the other side addressed them. "Mr. and Mrs. Whitfield, if you're ready, I'll escort you upstairs."

Alex returned the carton to its hiding place and held out his hand for Leila. She took it, feeling him lace his fingers through hers.

"Let's rewind 10 minutes and start over," he said close to her ear. "We're about to toast our new life together as we set sail across the ocean blue. No worries or silly disagreements. Only fun and romance from here on in. Got it?"

Leila was about to protest. She didn't think her reaction to his change of opinion 12 hours into being married was "silly", but Luca knocked louder this time. *Maybe it would be better if I dropped it*

Hand-in-hand, Leila and Alex made their way to the top deck. "Now this is living," Alex said as the yacht started to motor away from the island. He put his arm around Leila's shoulder and pulled her tightly against his side.

She had to admit that the sight was breathtaking and quite romantic. The lush green mountains of the Virgin Islands rose steeply out of the aquamarine water. She imagined what it must have been like before any modern development, when the first explorers stepped foot on the white sandy beaches.

"Champagne?" Luca asked, interrupting the couple's intimate moment.

"Sure," Leila answered and then watched the petite woman walk over to the bar situated under the covered corner of the deck.

Leila was about to comment to Alex about the quality of the expensive French bottle Luca set out when she heard a cell phone ringtone. It was Luca's. The woman looked at the number and then nervously glanced around. She turned away from the couple and answered quietly. Leila could barely hear the one-sided hushed conversation, but it was clear that Luca was trying to assure whoever was on the other end that she was on top of her job and the caller had nothing to worry about. Leila wondered if it was Maxim checking in to make sure their trip was off to a good start. When Luca said "Goodbye" and shoved the phone back into her pocket, Leila quickly averted her gaze. She didn't want to be caught eavesdropping.

Within moments Leila heard Luca walk up to them.

"Here you go," she said, handing each of them a crystal flute filled with the bubbling drink. After making sure they were satisfied, she excused herself, needing to check to see if the kitchen was ready serve breakfast.

"To my wife, the only woman I've ever known who is worth dying for," Alex said, tapping his glass to hers.

"Gee, I hope that's never the case," Leila added with a crooked smile. "How about we just toast to our future? May it be filled with great adventures, lots of surprises, and undying love."

"To our future," he repeated as they clinked their flutes together. After taking a sip, he bent down and kissed her on the lips.

Leila smiled. *It's all smooth sailing from this point on.*

CHAPTER EIGHTEEN

"Mom, get up," Jack's voice urged. "You have to see something! Quick!"

Sara was in a far away place, asleep. She was trapped. A dark, menacing figure reeking of liquor was hovering over her paralyzed body. She wanted to scream, to fight, to run but somewhere, somehow Jack was calling to her, shaking her free from this evening's prison.

"Wake up!" he said. "I have to show you what I found."

Sara's nightmare swirled away like water rushing down the bathtub drain. She pried open one eyelid and was assaulted by the morning light. She closed her eye, but it was too late. Jack knew she was awake and was insistent that she listen to him.

He tugged the blanket off her shoulder "Great. You're up."

"What time is it?" she whispered. She felt dehydrated and exhausted. She was certain a deranged farmer broke into the room overnight and stuffed her mouth full of cotton. She looked around at the unfamiliar surroundings and recalled they had wisely spent the night at the vineyard after the wedding reception. "Why are you up?"

"It's around eight o'clock, I guess. I slept in Alex's office, on the sofa last night, 'cause all the other beds were taken. Remember? It so stunk. And to top things off, this stupid bird has been flying into the window since dawn. I tried shooing it away, but the retarded thing keeps coming back."

"Jack Miller, we don't use the term retarded. It's not nice."

Jack rolled his eyes. "Geez, sor-ry!" he said, drawing the second syllable out with a snotty snap. "Anyway, that's not why I woke you up."

Sara decided she didn't have the energy to argue with her increasingly moody pre-teen. "So what is so darned important that you barged in here to drag me out of bed?" she asked.

"I didn't mean to peek, I swear, but I bumped into it and the box fell on the floor. The top came open and I couldn't help it. There she was. Mom, you have to come, please. It's important. I'm totally not kidding."

Sara was frustrated by his convoluted explanation. "Fine, I'll get up. Give me a minute to throw on my dress and I'll meet you in the hall."

Jack made a hasty exit, leaving her to slip back into the wrinkled gown she wore the night before. *Pantyhose. I don't think so,* she thought as she tossed the stockings across a chair. She snatched her watch from the nightstand. It read 8:17. She was glad she made arrangements for Carlos, their former farmhand, to drive over to take care of the horses and dogs an extra day. They could always count on him. Sara was sick when her trainer lured him away for twice the salary. But Carlos always went out of his way to help her if she ran into a snag.

Jack cracked the door open an inch. "Are you ready?"

Sara considered her high heels and made the rational decision. *Barefoot it is.* "Lead the way," she said, joining him in the chilly hallway.

They quietly made their way down to the first floor, careful to avoid a racket that might wake the other, still sleeping guests. As they entered Alex's office, Sara could hear the incessant tapping of a beak and wings against glass.

"It's over here, Mom," Jack explained, waving for her to hurry.

The noise abruptly stopped, making Sara come to a halt midway across the carpet. Curious, Sara detoured away from her son to see if the animal was lying on the frozen ground.

She knew that birds that catch their reflection will assume it's an interloper invading their territory and react aggressively, but they rarely die in the process. They're more likely to become temporarily stunned after a forceful collision. Sara peeked out the window, scanning the underbrush, but saw nothing more than a few black feathers. *Strange.*

"Mom," Jack said impatiently.

Sara gave into his urgings and turned her attention to Alex's desk. Boxes of wrapped wedding presents were stacked into precariously high piles. The couple didn't have time to open them before leaving on their honeymoon.

Jack yanked the top off one of the gifts. "Look!"

"Jack, what are you doing? You don't open up other people's stuff!"

"I told you already, I knocked it down by accident and the thing fell open. That's how I saw what was in it. I picked it up, stuck the top back on, then ran to get you."

Sara wasn't pleased, but she took a step forward to appease him. What she saw inside the box made her gasp.

"See, I told ya! It's totally weird...and sick."

"It's Leila," Sara said. She stared at a much younger painted version of her best friend. The portrait depicted Leila gazing over her shoulder. Long ebony hair fell to the middle of her naked back, suggesting she was posing nude for the artist. The expression was one that Sara recognized; it was the face of a seductress. Across the canvas a single word was scrawled in red marker: WHORE!

"Mom, who did this?" Jack asked.

"I don't know," Sara replied, feeling a knot tighten in her stomach. "Is there a card?"

"Not on the outside," he answered, flipping the top over to check.

"Check inside the box. Maybe it's stuck underneath," Sara suggested, not wanting to touch the disturbing image.

Jack lifted the oil painting out and showed Sara the back. The title and date were penned in black-inked calligraphy: *The Unrepentant Siren, December 1989.*

"What the...? We were freshmen in college in 1989. This is bizarre. Is there a signature on the front?"

Jack turned the oil painting back over. "The initials CAP are in the right corner, but who the heck is that?"

"I don't know, sweetie," Sara said, sighing. She grabbed the empty box and shook it, hoping to dislodge the answers, but nothing came. No card, no clues.

"What should we do? Auntie Leila is gonna freak when she sees this!"

"That would be putting it lightly. This is the plan. We're going to confiscate that disgusting thing and take it with us."

"Okay."

"Run it out to the car for me; I can't because I left my shoes upstairs," Sara said. "Be sure to stick it in the back under the extra horse blankets. I don't want anyone to see it. Whoever did this is not getting another chance to be cruel. I'm not about to leave it here for Leila and Alex to find when they get home."

Jack's eyes lit up with an angry protectiveness. "Mom, why would someone say this? Who hates Auntie Leila that much?"

"I wish I knew. Now scoot, before someone comes in here and catches us. I don't want to have to explain why we're making off with one of the presents."

Sara watched as Jack shoved the painting back into the box, then stealthily stole away with the noxious gift tucked under his arm. She glanced over at the window one last time before leaving. A cold chill made her shiver. *Who did this? Who painted you in '89? And who the hell is holding a grudge?* Ava's cautionary words about the soul-damaging dangers in choosing to withhold forgiveness rang true yet again. But what was more disturbing to Sara were the obvious coincidences that seemed to crop up around Leila and her new husband's family. The signs were adding up, gathering like storm clouds over an angry and dangerous sea, but Ava was clear that Sara needed to be patient and avoid interfering. According to the medium, fate needed to be allowed to unfold.

Leila was on her honeymoon and out of contact until the third week of January. In the meantime, Sara was determined to enlist a more experienced detective to dig into this mystery. Sara waited for Jack's thumbs-up before taking the next step. David was still asleep, snoring loudly under the thick, double-weave blanket. She sat down on the edge of the bed, wishing she was still tucked in snug-as-a-bug next to him versus chasing elusive shadows from the past. *Screw fate. The present situation demands attention.* Sara gently shook her husband. "David, wake up."

A moment later his eyes fluttered open. "What's the matter?"

"I need your help. Get dressed. We have to talk."

David stayed silent for a second, studying Sara. "This better be a matter of life or death," he eventually replied.

"I sure as hell hope not," Sara said.

CHAPTER NINETEEN

Leila and Alex spent the next week soaking up the yacht's over-the-top lavish lifestyle as it motored across the deep, blue waters of the Atlantic. They slept, ate and made love as they pleased, the crew ever-ready to bring them another bottle of wine or plate of caviar. The sundeck called to them in the mornings, luring them to bake their pale winter skin into a golden bronze. The evenings were spent soaking in the Jacuzzi, sipping French champagne and mapping out their future plans. The first leg on their long journey was about to come to an end with a stop-over in the Azores, a group of islands off the coast of Portugal. The Captain informed them at dinner that they would be dropping anchor sometime around seven o'clock in the morning, only 10 hours away.

"I've never been to the Azores, have you?" Leila asked Alex as she lazily lounged back on one of the deck chaises. She couldn't take her eyes off the stars overhead; they sparkled like living diamonds, dancing closer to the Earth with each radiant flicker.

Before he could answer, Luca cleared her voice behind them. She held a platter with a dozen bite-sized desserts: profiteroles, chocolate mousse cups, tiny tortes and petit popovers. "Sorry to interrupt," she said, setting them down on a small table between the newlyweds. "Eric was bringing up the bottle of Cristal, but one of the flutes tipped over and shattered. He went back to replace it. I apologize for the short delay. Is there anything else you require?"

"No. That will be all," Alex said.

"Very well," she replied. "Enjoy."

Eric passed her as she was dismissed. Leila noticed him drop his gaze; she imagined he felt embarrassed for being such a klutz.

"Madame, Monsieur," he said as he carefully set the tray down, then handed them each a glass filled with the bubbling wine.

"Merci," Leila said. She patiently waited for the young man to finish his duties. He plunged the open bottle into a nearby bucket filled with ice, nodded curtly, then strode away. Leila lifted her glass and made a toast. "Here's to casting our old lives to the wind and embracing our new life filled with exotic new lands and bold new adventures."

"I'll drink to that." Alex touched his flute to hers, took a long sip and loudly belched.

Leila giggled. "Nice, I see where this marriage is headed. Next you'll be farting and scratching your balls"

"Not me, my dear." He downed the rest of the glass in one quick gulp.

"Whoa, slow down. This stuff is meant to be savored."

"True, but I'm thirsty. Plus, I think the boat is pretty well stocked; it's not likely that we'll polish off the supply."

Leila watched as her husband popped two of the tiny desserts into his mouth and reached behind himself for the bottle on ice. She chose to let the liquid wash over her tongue slowly, allowing all the flavors to fully develop. Alex refilled his drink twice more before she was ready for him to pour her a second.

"Honey, you're spilling it. Be careful," Leila scolded Alex, as champagne trickled down the crystal stem and onto her hand.

"Sorry," he replied, groggily. "Wow, the alcohol has really hit me. I feel wasted."

Leila realized she was having a hard time focusing on his face. She rubbed her eyes with the palm of her hand and shook her head; it was no use, she still felt woozy. The sound of a loud thud made her look around. Alex was lying back with his mouth wide open and his eyes closed. The thick glass bottle was rolling across the deck, spilling the remaining liquid across the polished boards.

"Alex," she said, barely able to say his name without slurring. "Are you awake?"

He didn't move or make a sound. She prodded him with her foot, but he didn't stir.

Another noise caught her attention. The ship was making an unusual humming. She glanced around but didn't see Luca or Eric to ask what was happening. Curious, she tried to get up, but found the world was rotating at odd angles. Prone to stubbornness, even when drunk, she awkwardly zigzagged her way over to the railing. Deep male voices speaking in a foreign language floated up from the lower deck. The reflection of the moon off the ocean's surface made her realize that the yacht was at a standstill with the motor idling. Off the stern, she saw the lights of another ship bobbing in the distance. Halfway between the two, a small launch was speeding directly toward them. It was at that point that something sinister registered in her mind. She only drank one glass of champagne, but here she was straining to stay awake. Alex was out cold. They were drugged.

Panic ripped through her chest as she stumbled toward her unconscious husband. "Alex, Alex! You have to get up!"

There wasn't even a hint of a response. Leila was on her own.

The men's voices were getting closer and Leila was certain they were coming up the stairwell. Frantically, she scanned the deck for a way to flee. There was no escape. *Help! I need help...Sara.*

Leila checked her pockets and nearly cried. She left her cell phone in the room. They lost coverage days ago so she didn't bother carrying it around. In desperation, she searched Alex's pockets. Luckily, she found his cell, which was fully charged. "Thank God."

Adrenaline was pumping through Leila's veins, fighting back the effects of the drug. She stumbled toward the edge of the deck, trying to find a signal. The Azores were only a few hours away; maybe there was a chance. She punched in Sara's number and hit the send button, but the connection kept failing. Tears were welling up in her eyes as thoughts streamed through her mind. *Why is this happening? Are they pirates? Do they want a ransom?*

Leila backed against the safety railing; she knew the intruders would be upon them at any second. As if on cue, four men dressed in black appeared. They stopped next to Alex and shoved his shoulder. When they were positive he would offer no resistance, they turned their attention to Leila. She screamed, pressing send one last time. She felt herself become weaker. Fear pushed her to seriously consider jumping over the railing. With her judgment impaired by chemicals, she envisioned being able to impersonate James Bond by leaping to the next level and escaping on a jet ski. Tapping into her last reserves of energy and raw will to live, Leila threw the useless phone at the men and clumsily swung her leg over the edge. Momentum and the pull of gravity carried the rest of her body along the same path, plunging her into the darkness.

CHAPTER TWENTY

Cornrow braids of barren vines cut orderly lines across the bleak landscape. Snow flurries drifted down in slow motion, silencing whatever creatures weren't hibernating. Sara stood alone, staring at the single spot of color splattered against the gray background; the raven's blood spilled from its lethal wound, trickling like a woodland brook over the frozen turf. She was too late to alter the outcome, too late to save it.

The telephone next to the bed rang loudly, rousing Sara from a few hours of restless slumber. She was just getting her bearings when the silence was interrupted a second time. The alarm clock on the nightstand read 1:45 a.m. Sara felt for the handset but realized it wasn't on her side. The third ring made David moan in protest and cover his head with a pillow.

"Honey, answer it," Sara said. "It could be important."

"Who the hell would be calling at this time?" he asked angrily. Reluctantly, he turned over and picked up the phone. "It's coming up 'unknown' on the Caller-ID. It's probably a wrong number. Go back to sleep."

"David, for Pete's sake, see who it is."

He sighed and pressed the button. "Hello."

"What?" he asked.

Suddenly very cold, Sara shivered. It felt as if the needle on the thermometer dipped at least 15 degrees. She anxiously waited for her husband to say something else, but minutes passed before he uttered another word. When he abruptly sat up and turned on the light, she knew something terrible had happened.

"Yes, I understand," he said, his tone becoming very businesslike and serious. "I'll handle it on my end. Call us when you land." When he hung up, he avoided making eye contact with Sara.

"David, who the hell was on the phone?" she asked, her pulse already starting to race. Her heart told her what her brain was trying to deny: Something had happened to Leila. Sara watched him rub the back of his head. He took a deep breath then turned to look her in the face. "It was Alex."

At that moment she knew. She understood the dream right then. Sara started shaking as she held her breath waiting for the words.

"There was an accident."

"Oh, God, no!"

"Leila is missing. They were on a yacht nearing the Azores; I don't know, somewhere near Spain or Portugal. Alex said they've searched for her for days, but she's gone, presumed dead. Apparently, they were drunk, he passed out and she…well, who knows what she was doing? One of the crew members eventually woke him up after noticing blood and hair on the railing of a lower deck. If she went into the water drunk, bleeding and potentially unconscious in shark-infested waters, there would be little to no chance for her. Honey, the authorities have called a halt to the search. They don't think she'll ever be found."

"No, no, no!" Sara screamed.

David reached out and drew Sara into his arms, but her grief was too raw and overwhelming. She fought against him, repeatedly striking out as she gasped for air between stilted sobs. Fifteen minutes went by before she collapsed against his chest, her energy spent and her faith slipping away. He held her for a long time, stroking her hair in silence.

"What's Alex going to do now?" Sara asked, emotionless.

"He's catching a flight back. He should be landing at Dulles in the morning."

"What does he want you to do?"

David gazed down at her as he lifted her chin. "Obviously, he wanted me to tell you, but he also asked if we could call Leila's brother and father. I don't think he has the strength to relive the details over and over again to everyone that needs to be informed. I think he's harboring a fair amount of guilt."

"Why, because he was asleep?" Sara asked.

"As far as he's concerned, he wasn't there to help her when she needed him the most."

I know the feeling, Sara thought.

"He asked if you could see if Tom might be up to leading a memorial service in the next week or two. He really felt like Leila would prefer Tom. He's family."

Sara started to cry again. Anger surfed along the crest of her emotions until it came crashing through unfettered. "How the fuck could this happen? The railings on ships aren't low. It takes effort to fall overboard."

David opened his mouth to say something, but then paused.

Sara noticed and didn't let him get away with it. "What else?"

He averted his eyes as he shared Alex's theory. "When he passed out, his cell phone was in his pocket, but when he woke, it was on the other side of the deck. Alex checked the last number dialed." David swallowed hard before revealing the rest. "There were several calls to us the evening she disappeared. He thinks she was trying to phone you but couldn't get a signal."

Sara shook her head, not wanting to hear the rest.

"In a drunken daze, she most likely concocted the bright idea to climb up on the railing. Can't you picture her balancing up there, trying to get a connection and then one slip, one tilt this way or that, and the cell flies one direction and she tumbles the other?"

"Oh, Leila," was all Sara could say. Guilt and sorrow dissolved her footing, drowning her in a sea of her own salty tears.

Sleep was elusive the rest of the night. Sara finally slipped into a dreamless void around dawn. Jack's voice woke her up a few hours later.

"Mom, where's Dad?" he asked.

"Huh?" she mumbled, still half-asleep. "I don't know. Why?"

"I need to talk to you alone," he whispered. Jack poked his head into the master bath, then closed the bedroom door.

Sara pushed herself up against the headboard. The t-shirt she wore was still damp from tears. She wanted to rip it off in an effort to destroy the evidence that last night was real and that she wasn't having another nightmare, but it would have to wait. Jack was demanding her full attention. "What do you need to tell me?" she asked.

"I had a dream," he explained, gesturing wildly with his hands. "But it was like totally real. I was awake and this lady was there in my room talking to me and then when she was done, 'poof,' she was gone."

Sara's interest was piqued. "Go on."

"She wants me to give you a message. She told me it was a matter of life or death. This isn't what she wants; he misunderstood."

"Who?"

"Charlie," Jack said.

"So, the lady wants me to do something about Charlie?" Sara asked, completely confused.

"No," he said, impatiently. "The lady's name is Charlie. She wants you to touch the painting, the one we brought home from Auntie Leila's wedding. She said you will understand. She's gonna show you."

Sara's mind reeled as she thought about the "present" she safely tucked away on the top shelf of her closet. The prickly feeling on the back of her neck sent an army of goosebumps charging down to the tips of her limbs. "C-A-P...Charlie?"

"And Mom, she said to please hurry. Oh, and one more thing. Shoot, what was it? Oh yeah, yeah...to have faith."

Faith, Sara thought. *That's what Ava told me, to have faith in our connection. Oh God, what if Leila's still alive!*

Sara lunged out of bed and ran to the closet. Standing on her tiptoes, she hit the corner of the box, sending it tumbling to the carpet. It landed with a thud and spilled open. Sara stared down into the face of her best friend, the same woman she grieved for all night long. The thought of holding the painting was unnerving, but there was no choice. Sara sat on the floor trembling as her finger traced the curve of Leila's bare shoulder. Contact with the canvas instantly opened a door, transporting her to another place in time.

"Come on, Charlie. Let me see!" Leila said, pleading her case over her shoulder. She was sitting on a stool with her back toward the artist. Sara was mesmerized by the scene. The late afternoon light streamed through the windows, illuminating the young woman's naked skin so that it appeared to have a radiant glow. Leila's face was frozen in an irresistibly seductive trance; there wasn't a hint of self-consciousness in her erotic pose.

"I'm almost done," Charlie replied, with a sugary-sweet accent.

The voice grabbed Sara's attention. She watched the young woman smile as she considered her magnificent work. Sara glanced at the girl on the canvas and compared it to the three-dimensional version perched on the other side of the room in all her glory. It was a perfect match. The artist used

*the brush to add "CAP" at the bottom of the picture, then
stood up and stretched. She was a beauty in her own right
with long golden locks, sparkling eyes, and an athletic body.
Sara was transfixed by her pixie-like face; it reminded her of
someone, but who?*

"Now you can take a look," the artist said, slyly.

*Leila bolted from her seat, not bothering to cover up.
"Wow! Charlie you're amazing. That is really good!"*

Charlie blushed. "It's easy when you're the model."

*Sara stepped to the side, watching as Leila couldn't take
her eyes off the portrait and Charlie couldn't take her eyes
off a naked Leila.*

*"What does the A stand for?" Leila asked, pointing to
her signature.*

*"It's a family name. Kind of sucks for a middle name, but
my mother got her way when I was born. It's Ashton."*

*"Charlie Ashton Powers, you are one hell of a talented
artist," Leila stated, bouncing up and down with delight. "I
have the coolest roommate on campus."*

"Charlie Ashton Powers…Charlotte Ashton Powers.
Holy…I thought she died when she was a little girl. Alex
never told me the whole story," Sara said aloud, but neither
girl heard a sound. She didn't exist in their world.

*"What if I wanted to be more than an artist and your
roommate?" Charlie asked, moving closer to touch her
muse's shoulder with her paint-stained fingers.*

Leila turned her head, "What do you mean?"

*Charlie reached up and gently brushed the hair from
Leila's cheek. "I think you know."*

*Sara couldn't believe her eyes, but Leila still didn't
understand. It took Charlie gliding forward to kiss her in one
swift and fluid motion for the artist's words to make sense.*

*Leila's body tensed, hesitating long enough for Charlie's
hands to wander down the small of her back. When Leila*

tried to step away, Charlie held tight, refusing to let go.

"Stop it," Leila demanded, when she pulled her lips free. "What are you doing?"

"I can't...I love you," Charlie said, letting this confession spill over like a rushing waterfall. "I know you feel the same way. I've seen the way you check me out when we're alone, the way your eyes follow me. See?" she argued, pointing to the painting. "You can't deny that look. You want me as bad as I want you. I understand...you're scared; I am too."

Leila pushed hard on Charlie's shoulders, forcing her back several feet. "No, I'm not and no, I don't! Holy crap, I can't believe you think I'm into you. You're crazy! Believe me, I like guys...exclusively," she said as she ran across the room and grabbed her clothes.

As Leila put them on, Charlie followed her, begging her to be truthful. "I know you don't mean it. I know deep down this is what you want. Please, give us a chance." Tears were starting to well up in the girl's eyes.

"Charlie, get this through your head: There is no us. Zip, zero, nada! I'm not a lesbian. We're friends and that's it. You asked me to model and I agreed. You told me to be seductive and I was, but I didn't do it to seduce you, I swear. If you got the wrong idea, I'm really sorry. We're roommates, but if you truly feel like this, I think it would be better for both of us if we request a change for next semester." Leila swung her purse over her shoulder and headed for the door.

"Wait. Don't go." Charlie sounded panicked.

Leila didn't even give her a second glance.

Charlie crumpled to the floor, dropping her head into her hands.

The scene was hard to watch. Sara wanted to break the connection and return to the closet, but clearly Charlie wasn't done showing her the past.

The weeping girl rose, walked over to a supply table and

picked up a pair of sharp scissors. Sara remembered Alex explaining his sister was dead. Was she about to witness the girl's suicide? Instinctively, Sara sprang forward in an attempt to swipe the shears from Charlie. As if she were a ghost from the future, her hand sliced harmlessly through the blades. She held her breath as the distraught teen brought them to her throat, but instead of hurting herself, she chopped off all her hair. Sara was stunned as the girl's beautiful blonde locks drifted to the ground, leaving behind a short, ragged mop. When done with her impromptu make-over, the young woman turned and looked Sara directly in the eye. In an instant, she recognized the girl within the woman; she was the same child from Alex's dated photograph. Not only that, Sara suspected that Charlotte was the apparition who appeared in the garden when Maxim was agitated about the mysterious paintbrush.

"Mom, you okay?" Jack asked, shaking her hard. The movement jarred her finger away from the painting. "You didn't answer me."

Sara felt disoriented, as if her mind was shuffling and realigning reality so she could function in the present.

"What did you see in there?"

"I found out who painted the picture, but I still don't know who wrote those words or who sent it." *Or if Leila is still alive*, she thought.

"Touch it again," he urged. "Maybe she'll show you the rest."

Her curiosity was piqued, although it was a completely disconcerting and uncomfortable experience, akin to being thrust head-first into a cold lake. After inhaling deeply, Sara took the plunge, taking hold of the portrait once more.

This time, Sara found herself in the backseat of a boat-sized station wagon. It was the kind with exterior wood paneling that thankfully disappeared by the late-eighties.

Charlie, her short locks dyed charcoal, was sitting behind the wheel with an adolescent version of Maxim at her side. A tiny ball of black fur with pointed ears was curled on the seat between the two siblings. In the dark, Sara didn't immediately recognize their location but the smell of salt water and vaporous mist signaled their proximity to the ocean. Towering live oak trees adorned with wispy Spanish moss lined the roads and bicycle paths. The weeping canopy and low-lying fog seemed to be the perfect backdrop for their ghostly adventure. After driving through part of a golf course, Charlie turned the car down a quiet, dead-end street. She pulled up to a house at the end of the cul-de-sac and turned off the ignition.

"Daddy is gonna be so surprised that we convinced Mama to let us drive out here tonight," Maxim said. "I can't wait for the sun to rise. Let's go sailing."

"Whatever," Charlie replied.

"You want your art stuff out?" he asked, climbing out of the car.

"Nah, I'll get it tomorrow," she answered.

Maxim opened the rear hatch to retrieve their duffle bags. "I'll get these. You go ahead."

"Come on, Reggie," Charlie said, setting the tiny pup on the ground.

Sara scooted through the car door, not needing to actually open it. The sound of waves crashing in the distance suggested the house was sitting near the beach, if not on it. She followed closely on Charlie's heels as the young woman made her way up the wooden steps to the typical Southern wrap-around porch. The front door was bolted. Clearly frustrated by not having the key, Charlotte stomped around to the side of the house. Suddenly, Sara felt an odd and disconcerting tugging at her skin, the unexpected sensation of having her psychic-shadow pass through Charlie's now-

still form. An untimely lapse of concentration let Sara miss the fact that the girl came to an abrupt halt next to a window. Inside, flickering candlelight cast long shadows against the walls as Nat King Cole crooned "Unforgettable" from the stereo. Sara heard Charlie catch her breath. The scene unfolding inside shook Sara to the core. Standing next to a couch, a half-dressed, middle-aged man was lip-locked with a much younger woman.

Max and Reggie came up the stairs, making a fair amount of racket with the luggage. Even with the warning, the couple was oblivious to the onlookers spying from the porch.

"What are you doing?" Maxim asked as he approached.

"Shush!" Charlie scolded, pointing.

The boy set the bags down before investigating what had his sister on the verge of exploding into a hissy-fit. "Who the...?"

At that moment, the mismatched couple seemed to take their cue to part, giving the small audience a glimpse of who was standing on the other side of that kiss. She wore a short, red sundress that complimented her suntanned skin and long dark hair. In one quick gesture, Ralston stripped her of the unnecessary frock, exposing a black lace ensemble that made Sara envision a model stepping off the pages of a 'Victoria's Secret' catalog.

Sara shook her head in disbelief. Leila? she whispered.

Apparently she wasn't the only one who saw the uncanny resemblance. When the couple entwined and collapsed onto the couch, it sent Charlie over the edge. The girl slammed the glass with the palms of both hands. "No!" she screamed. "You whore! Leila, how could you?"

Maxim's mouth fell open as he watched his sister flee to the car in tears. Before he could react, she recklessly backed out of the driveway and sped away, leaving young Maxim to deal with the inevitable aftermath.

The thunderous crack on the window brought Ralston running outside. "What the hell?" He was shocked to find his son standing on the porch.

"Charlotte saw you," Maxim said flatly. "She's gone."

"Gone? Where?"

Maxim's eyes narrowed into angry slits. "Home, I suppose. Isn't Mama gonna be surprised? I guess it's a night full of 'em."

Sara saw the older man turn a color usually reserved for the sick and dying.

Ralston ran inside, flicked on the light switch and urgently mumbled something to his confused date while gesturing for her to leave. It was obvious he was in a tremendous hurry as he fought to get a polo shirt over his head. A moment later he burst outside, grabbed hold of Maxim's elbow and yanked with threatening force. "This did not happen. Do you understand me? You saw nothing, no one. You will not breathe a word of this to your mother. If your sister even hints about what she saw, I swear I'll have her recommitted. We will not discuss this again…ever."

Maxim offered no response other than stone silence.

Ralston left the boy seething, alone in the darkness, as he tore away after his daughter in his silver Corvette convertible.

Sara remained there long enough to see the young seductress slip her dress back on and pull her hair into a neat ponytail, exposing the back of her graceful neck. "Oh my God! It's not there. How is that possible? Unless…."

Sara was still sorting out the unlikely reality she was witnessing in her mind when Maxim turned toward the window. As he watched the woman sneak out of the house, he hissed, "Leila."

CHAPTER TWENTY-ONE

The pain was excruciating as the drugs started to wear off. With nothing but complete darkness around her, Leila was certain she was dead; the only thing she didn't understand was why she was feeling such intense pain. She tried to move, but every muscle screamed out in angry protest. Involuntarily, she let out a whimper.

Where she was, how many hours, days, or weeks had passed and what had happened to her were all unanswered questions. As she lay still, trying to quell a firestorm of emotions, hazy images swam through her mind: being on the ship with Alex, the men boarding the boat, her husband drugged and unresponsive and her desperate attempt to flee. Leila's ill-thought-out leap landed her on the lower deck in a broken heap. She remembered the smart snap of her collar bone and the taste of blood on her tongue. Determined, she had tried to stand up, but her ankle refused to bear any weight.

Leila's last bit of fight bubbled to the surface when the largest of the captors threw her small frame over his shoulder. She wriggled so violently, he almost dropped her.

One of the others stormed over, slapped her hard, then brutally grabbed her bleeding face. "You don't want to make this more difficult, believe me," he said in stilted English.

As they carried her across the deck to the waiting speedboat, Luca and Eric passed, carrying duplicates of the champagne and desserts served a short time earlier. Luca gave her a sympathetic smile but did nothing to intervene. It was then that Leila realized they were only after her; Alex would wake from his drug-induced slumber and have no idea what happened. Leila was on her own, cold, broken and trapped in her nightmare.

A spontaneous eruption of intense fear bled into a deep and overpowering sorrow. Lying in her black prison, she began to weep. The salt of her tears was a reminder that she was still in fact alive. *Where am I? Alex, don't give up on me. Find me, please, wherever I am.* But what could he think? All the evidence would suggest she fell overboard and drowned. The crew would reinforce the idea. Why would he keep searching? Those thoughts were paralyzing. But out of the darkness, she found a glimmer of hope: *Sara*. Sara would know she was alive. Leila would make her feel it. She clung to the only thing she could, her faith in her best friend. She was certain Sara's tenacious nature, her unique ability to pick up on Leila's thoughts and her spot-on intuition would combine and ride to the rescue. But it had to be soon.

The sound of metal sliding against metal quickened her pulse. A crack of light streamed into the room as the door opened, causing her to instinctively shut her eyes and pretend to be asleep.

"No change. She's out cold," a man said, pushing roughly against her shoulder. He reeked of cigar smoke and vodka. "Lucky bitch lived."

Leila winced in pain, but thankfully, the men missed it.

A second man spoke up. "We'll be docking soon. Less trouble for us if she stays this way. As long as she's alive, we'll get paid."

"You know what's to be done with her?"

"Your guess is as good as mine. You know the drill. The more powerful the individual, the more twisted the payback is in the end."

Ice ran though her veins as she listened to their conversation. She was stuck knee-deep in a quagmire of quicksand. *Who the hell are you talking about? It was Maxim's boat. Could it be him? But why?*

"Seems a shame to waste the bitch," the first captor said,

letting his fingers brush across her breast. "Want a turn?"

Leila froze. She was in no condition to fight back. Her worst nightmare was going to come true: She was going to be raped.

"Sorry, I like my women awake," the second guy answered. "What fun is it when they don't even know what's happening? It's better when you see the terror in their eyes and when they beg for their pathetic lives."

A third voice crackled to life in the room. From the sound of it, Leila guessed one of the men was wearing a two-way radio. They were speaking in a foreign language. The back and forth lasted a minute or two, then the man switched back to English.

"The Captain wants us on deck."

"Damn it!"

"You'll have to save it for the next slut we kidnap."

The door slammed, casting her back into desolate isolation, but she didn't care; luck intervened on her behalf. *But what about next time? Sara, you have to save me. Please hurry.*

~

Sara sprinted through the house in search of her husband. With no trace of him, she reasoned he was at the barn, probably telling Emma the horrible, and inaccurate, news. But if they didn't act quickly, the window to rescue Leila would close. It was imperative that they enlist Alex's help immediately, but it wasn't going to be easy. Charlotte had shown her the final scene – and it tied all the strings together. Feeling the press of time, Sara bolted out the back door to the stables. "What time was Alex landing?" Sara asked, gasping for air.

David and Emma turned when they heard her voice.

They mirrored each other's worried expression. There was no doubt what they were thinking: A grief-addled, insane woman was on the loose.

Sara took stock of her appearance and condition: short nightshirt, barefoot, unwashed and uncombed running across gravel in 15 degree, blustery weather. They would have to get over it, and fast. "It's not true," Sara blurted out. "She's not dead. We have to convince Alex."

She could tell that her words weren't getting it done because this time David gave Emma a concerned, knowing glance.

Tears started to roll down Emma's pink cheeks. "I'm so sorry, Sara. This must be completely devastating for you. Is there anything I can do, anything at all?"

"She's alive," Sara insisted.

"Come on, honey," David said, taking off his coat and draping it around her shoulders. "Let's get you back to the house."

"Stop it! I need you to listen to me. I'm not imagining this."

David bent over and gently scooped Sara into his arms before she realized his intention.

"Let me go!" she yelled, smacking him in the chest with her fist.

"When we get inside," he replied. "Sorry. There will be no tempting fate to push you into a grave alongside Leila. At least not on my watch."

Sara saw Emma sadly shake her head, wipe the tears from her face and go back to work.

By the time they entered the kitchen, Sara could feel the steam ready to shoot from her ears.

David dumped her onto a stool and quickly stepped an arm's-length away from his fuming wife. "Honey, you need to calm down."

Sara was on the verge of letting loose a colorful string of expletives when Jack appeared, carrying the painting in his arms.

"Did you tell him?" he asked with boyish animation. "Can you believe it, Dad? The lady showed mom what happened."

David shot Sara a disapproving smirk, one that told her he didn't appreciate Jack being dragged into the middle of her delusions.

"Sara…," he said in a tone that clearly spelled out a warning.

Sara inhaled slowly, then released a deep, cleansing breath. There was a mountain to climb before enlisting Alex in her plan, and that treacherous peak was called Mt. David. "No, Jack. I'm about to tell your father now."

"Dad, it was so cool," Jack said.

Sara smiled at David, who left no doubt about his skepticism

"Charlie told me to get mom to hold the painting," Jack explained, gesturing wildly, "…and when she did, Wham! It was like one of those time portal thingies or like that big vat of memories from the Harry Potter movies. Tell him, Mom."

"We're all aware that you hate when something from the other side comes knocking, but if we don't listen, Leila is going to end up dead," Sara said. "Please, trust me."

David shut his eyes and rubbed them, as if that would erase the implausibility of the tale he was hearing. "I give up. Tell me what you think you saw."

Sara knew she won the first battle. When she was done conveying the content of her visions, she hopped off her seat and went over to him. "I need your help. She's alive; I'm one hundred percent certain. I've been having the same nightmare for months. She's locked in a room, alone in the dark, but she won't be for long. He's on his way to get her as we speak."

"And where exactly is that?" David asked, sounding exasperated. "She disappeared in the middle of the frigging ocean. If Leila is alive, and that is a huge 'if,' she could be anywhere in the world by now. And who is 'he?'"

"That's why we need Alex. I have to tell him what happened. The truth has to come out."

David laughed. "Really? You think he's going to buy into this Technicolor fantasy? Forget it; the poor grief-stricken bastard is going to throw you out on your tight little ass."

"He has to believe me or we'll never find her," Sara argued, slipping closer to a state of panic. She could feel her heart racing and her palms getting sweaty.

Jack thrust the canvas in his parents' direction. "Show him the painting…the signature. If his sister was the artist, he'll recognize it and he'll believe what you're telling him."

Sara thought it was a brilliant idea. "Jack, you're a genius! I'm getting dressed. I'll be ready to go in 10 minutes."

David rolled his eyes in defeat. "I'll meet you in the car."

CHAPTER TWENTY-TWO

The vineyard was closed to the public for the month of January. The place was scaled back, running with a skeleton staff.

When Sara and David arrived, Louie greeted them at the door. "Hey, David."

"Lou," David replied somberly as he shook the man's hand. "Sorry to intrude."

Louie kissed Sara on the cheek then led the couple into the house's foyer. "No problem, come on in. I guess you've heard about Leila. Such a terrible tragedy."

"That's why we're here," Sara explained. *To prevent it from getting much worse.*

"Alex just got home. He's in his office opening wedding presents, of all things," Louie said, pointing to the box Sara held in her arms. "I think he's losing it."

Sara's heart broke as she pictured the bereaved man sifting through each gift that was supposed to usher in a joyful future with his new wife.

"We need to talk to him," David said. "It can't wait."

"It's at your own risk. The guy is a jagged and raw wound." He patted David on the shoulder for luck and hastily parted company, leaving the couple to confront Alex alone.

"You're sure about this?" David asked. "'Cause if you're wrong, you might send him over the edge. Don't create any false hope."

"I'm not going to do that. Leila was taken," Sara confidently insisted.

"If you're right, it doesn't really turn out much better, does it? To have your wife kidnapped by a member of your own family? The poor guy is totally screwed either way."

Sadly, Sara nodded in agreement. "Knock."

David did as she asked.

"Go away," Alex yelled from the other side of the door.

David looked to his wife for direction. She signaled to David to open the wooden door. When they entered, an obstacle course of scattered debris lay across the room. Shattered crystal vases, china plates and wine decanters were intermingled with torn cardboard, tissue paper and wrapping. It was a war zone, fraught with battered and beaten love. Alex was behind his desk, filling a glass with scotch. Sara glanced at her watch. It was only 11 a.m.

"Alex," Sara said, softly.

"I can't do this," Alex answered, wiping away an angry tear. "Get out."

Sara wasn't sure whether or not they should take cover in case he started lobbing things.

"Hey, man, we know you're dying inside, but if this wasn't important, we wouldn't be here," David explained, hesitating for a second. "It's about Leila...she may be alive."

Alex swung his gaze away from his drink and dropped it like a heavy lead cannonball on top of David. "What the hell are you saying? Leila is gone."

"It's supposed to appear that way so you would give up, but she's not," Sara said quickly, as if the words might be stolen from her mouth if she didn't get them out. "I would never joke about this...ever. She was, is, my best friend."

Alex shook his head.

"I was there," he recalled aloud. "I reacted the same way; I didn't believe it at first either. I told them 'no, she's alive.' I was in denial. It was pathetic; I couldn't wrap my brain around the truth. Have a drink. It helps." Alex gulped the liquid and slammed down the glass.

"I'm not in denial and this is no fictional story I concocted to make me feel better," Sara said firmly. "I need to show you something. I took this out of here the morning after the wedding. I didn't want you to see it, but now there's no choice. There's a message attached, one that is going to save your wife's life." Sara dropped the box in front of Alex and lifted the lid.

He stared at it without saying a word.

"Do you recognize the signature on the bottom, CAP?" she asked.

"Charlotte," he whispered.

"Did you know that Charlotte and Leila were roommates in college, before your father committed your sister to a psychiatric hospital to 'fix' her depression and 'identity' confusion?" Sara didn't want to have to say out loud the dirty details of Leila's connection with Alex's family. She was hoping to make Alex connect the dots.

"No," he replied, shaking his head. "They…I…."

"Did you know that the other members of your family recognized Leila from the past?"

"What? No."

Sara realized the inevitable; Alex had no clue. She took a deep breath and continued. "Yes, it's true. The summer after this was painted your father brought a woman back to his house in Hilton Head for a romantic interlude. She was a lovely, tempting young thing with a remarkably familiar face and long dark hair."

"It can't be," Alex said.

"Your father thought they were alone. Unfortunately, your siblings arrived in time to put two-and-two together."

"I can't hear this! Stop it! Shut up!" Alex closed his eyes and shook his head violently.

Sara knew she couldn't ease up now or she would lose him. "Your sister was devastated by what she saw. She was in love with Leila; you can see it in the detailed beauty of the painting. A brief glimpse of the woman your father held in his embrace led her to assume the worst. She fled to Charleston with her emotions running wild, but she was tragically mistaken. Even though the woman resembled Leila in almost all respects, she had no birthmark on the back of her neck. It was someone else."

"This is insane!" Alex yelled. "You would have no way of knowing any of this."

"Your father followed Charlotte, fearful that she would tell your mother about the affair and terrified that a scandal would bring down his fledgling political career," Sara continued, without acknowledging his protests. "All of the elements of a catastrophic confrontation were in play. When your father arrived home, he found Charlotte, who was going by the name of Charlie, alone in the carriage house."

"No," Alex said.

"Sara, tread lightly," David whispered, clearly concerned for Alex's state of mind.

Unfortunately, Sara knew all too well there was no shortcut through the lies. "After leaving the hospital, your sister turned the building into a makeshift studio. It was filled with her artwork: charcoal sketches, watercolor garden scenes, grand oils of boats sailing in the harbor and portraits... lots and lots of portraits with one dominant theme: Leila. She made reprints of the original painting you have in your hands: large ones, small ones, close ups. She was completely obsessed; not an uncommon characteristic for first loves by any means. So as you can imagine, she was already in a very agitated state when your father discovered her. You can see the outrage scrawled across the canvas in front of you. But, the hateful words weren't enough; she grabbed a utility knife and started slashing everything in the building. When she saw your dad standing in the doorway, it only magnified and concentrated her rage. In her eyes, he was the one that kept her away from Leila. Without giving a damn, he tarnished the object of her desire. He spoiled her fantasy and her life; now, she wanted to destroy his world in return."

Alex was shocked. He sat with his mouth agape and motionless as he listened to the twisted tale of the destruction of his family.

"Still holding the exposed blade, Charlotte tried to run past him," Sara gently said. "She was going to tell your mother what she saw. She was planning to expose him, but she didn't make it. He caught her by the hair and demanded that she stop, saying, 'Where do you think you're going?' I experienced the same thing while staying at your family's home in Charleston. Thankfully, I got out alive, but your sister didn't. When he pulled her backwards, she swung around in a hysterical frenzy. There was a bitter struggle. I think he was caught off guard by the intensity of her reaction. As he was trying to pry the knife from her hands, they tripped and the blade…." Sara paused briefly, sympathetic to the pain she was causing. "Well it…it sliced through her throat, severing her carotid artery. She bled out before his eyes."

"Why are you telling me this?" Alex asked, choking on the tears that were streaming freely down his ruddy cheeks. He swiped at them with the backs of his hands, but there was no stemming the flow. "Charlotte's been gone for a long time. It's cruel."

"Because," Sara explained, swallowing hard, "…because those series of events led to your family dissolving. Your sister's death was covered up as a suicide while your father's guilt ate away at him like termites infesting a rotting log. The loss drove your mother to the slippery edge of insanity. In the end, without knowing the full story, she came to blame your father anyway. The tragedy culminated in their divorce, and your little brother was privy to what lit the fuse that blew it all up. A couple of decades later you stroll in with the same destructive siren on your arm. You lit the fuse, but this time, it was to a plot of revenge."

"What are you saying?" Alex asked, "That my family harbored some kind of vendetta against my wife for more than 20 years? You're the one who's crazy."

"Leila didn't fall overboard and drown. She was kidnapped and is alive…for now."

Alex's expression shifted as sorrow morphed into incredulous disbelief. The man could have been slapped across the face and he wouldn't have appeared any more stunned. He turned his attention to David. "You're going along with this nonsense? She's lost her mind. Well, either that or she's the most sadistic person I've ever met."

David's gaze dropped to the floor. He didn't reply.

"I'm neither," Sara insisted, sticking up for herself.

"Yeah, then where's your proof? How do you know any of this, huh? Tell me!"

"Your sister showed me," Sara said, knowing he would balk at her response. "I've been getting signs ever since Leila's first accident – premonitions, glimpses of memory and direct contact by your sister's restless spirit. That painting came into my hands for a reason. Your sister, Charlotte, was desperate for me to understand. She found a way to reveal the past and uncover the truth, so we could intervene to change Leila's future."

Alex lifted the portrait from its box, stood up and strode angrily to the other side of his desk. "You want me to believe this painting spoke to you, told you that my father, mother, brother – hell, maybe even Charlotte – abducted my wife off a ship in the middle of the ocean to exact some kind of revenge for…what? A case of mistaken identity?"

Sara wasn't sure she was going to be able to turn this around. He was hell-bent on thinking she was fabricating the entire story. "It's not uncommon to try to find a scapegoat when life collapses in a heap at your feet. In this case, it was the girl who kept showing up at the center of the conflicts. The paintings left behind a reminder; they seared her face into memory, accurate or not. I'm not even sure your father realizes that the woman he was kissing in his beach house all those years ago was not the same one as depicted over and over again in oil paint."

"This theory is entirely ridiculous. Plus, my mother destroyed all Charlotte's artwork except the first floral watercolor that hangs in her old bedroom," Alex said, adamantly arguing his point.

"Obviously, she did not. The proof is in your hands."

Alex transferred his bitter gaze from Sara to the haunted canvas.

"Hey, I didn't see that before," David added, stepping forward to get a better look. "What's that on the back?"

"The title of the portrait," Sara replied. Alex flipped it over as the phrase left Sara's lips. "The Unrepentant Siren."

"No, no, no!" Alex said with increasing intensity. "This can't be."

"What?" David asked.

Alex was trembling with rage as he spat the words out. "It's the name of the yacht we were on. Maxim, you son of a bitch!" It was like pulling a pin on a grenade; he spun around, beating the painting against the edge of his desk until the only thing left was splinters and ribbons. With an anguished cry, he threw the remnants across the room.

Sara and David backed off during Alex's reckoning with reality. Sara whispered in David's ear, "We need to find that yacht. The crew might know where they took her."

"What about your suspicions about his father and the conversation you overheard at the reception?" David said quietly. "How does he fit in?"

"I don't know, but we have a definite lead with the boat."

"You think he can see through this shit-storm to be helpful?" David asked, nodding in Alex's direction.

"I'm counting on it. Give him a few more minutes." Sara's cell phone interrupted their musings, chirping away like a cheerful songbird in her purse. She checked the incoming number. It was from Sean, her biological father. He was abroad for the last couple of months, but the last leg of his journey came to a bittersweet end that morning when his cruise ship sailed into Fort Lauderdale, Florida.

"It's Sean. I'll call him back later," she said, stuffing it unanswered back into its small leather pouch.

Sara's words captured Alex's attention, cutting through the noose of emotion that was surely strangling him. "No, answer it. Tell him to say a prayer for Leila…for us."

Sara was hesitant, but obliged. "I'll make it quick; time is of the essence. We need to start brainstorming about how to locate that yacht." She pressed the button and lifted the phone to her ear. "Hello."

"Hello, dear. It's so good to hear your voice!" Sean said, yelling across the line as if she couldn't get a clear connection from so far away.

"How was the trip?" she asked.

Sean chuckled. "Splendid, wonderful, out of this world! Take your pick. The cruise was the icing on the cake. And speaking of cake, I think I gained 25 pounds. They sure do feed you on these excursions."

"That's great, Sean," Sara replied, impatiently. She felt bad she couldn't be more enthusiastic, but there were more pressing matters to deal with at the moment.

"I'm taking a stroll around the marina here, thought I could work off a calorie or two before the flight home. You should see all the gorgeous boats; they're just magnificent. They must be owned by movie stars."

"I guess."

"I tried your brother at the parish house but didn't get an answer," he said. "Thought for sure he would be in this time of day. I really missed him…and you, of course."

"Oh," Sara said. "I'm surprised too. Listen, there's so much to tell you, and not all good, but I don't have the time right now. We're dealing with a…."

"A what?" he asked, interrupting her.

"Well," Sara answered, not sure how to explain their predicament, "A crisis with Leila. She's missing. She disappeared on her honeymoon; vanished off some mega-yacht called 'The Unrepentant Siren' off the coast of the Azores. Please say a prayer for her. She's probably in a good bit of danger." The retired priest was silent so long that Sara thought the connection was dropped. "Hello, Sean? Are you there?"

"What did you say the name of the boat was?" he asked.

"'The Unrepentant Siren.' Why?"

"Now isn't that a darn coincidence? I don't have my distance glasses on, but I could swear that yacht is docked in one of the slips over on the other side of the marina. It's one of those big ones that don't fit in a regular parking spot."

"Oh my God, you're kidding me," she blurted out.

"Sara, it's a sin to use the Lord's name in vain," he scolded, always falling back on being mindful of God's rules and expectations.

"I know, but it's a miracle. We have to get to that boat."

"Is it there?" David asked. "Does he see it?"

Sara nodded.

"Sean, can you do us a favor? Can you stay around the area and keep an eye on the boat? We're going to catch the next flight down to Fort Lauderdale. If there's even the slightest hint that the thing is getting ready to move, call the police…no, the Coast Guard."

"And tell them what?" he asked.

"I don't know, ah...that they're drug smugglers. Be creative, anything to prevent them from leaving. I'll call you as soon as we land." Sara hung up and faced the two men.

"The Siren was heading to Italy," Alex said. "It shouldn't be in Florida."

"There are a whole lot of shouldn'ts when it comes to this situation. I'm banking on Sean," Sara replied. "We have to intercept that yacht before it sails again."

"Any idea where Maxim is right now?" David asked.

"I'm not sure," Alex answered. "He came to the Azores to help with the search but left on business when I flew back to the States."

"What about your father?" Sara asked.

"No, I haven't spoken to him. Max contacted my parents to tell them what happened to Leila. I was too upset. He's probably in the office."

"Call them," David stated. "It's fishing, but you never know. Make something up, like you're planning the memorial service and want to know if they can make it to Virginia the day after tomorrow. Find out what their schedule is like."

Alex nodded. He picked up the phone and punched in the first number. After a minute or two, it rolled over into voicemail. "Hey, Max. Get back to me as soon as you can."

He dialed again, this time to his father's office. "Hey, Sandy, it's Alex. Is my dad busy? ...I see, and he's gone for how long? No message. I'll catch up with him when he returns."

"What did she say?" Sara asked.

"He's out of town for the next few days on urgent out of state business," Alex explained through tight lips. "He didn't give her any other details."

"Try your mother," Sara said. "Maybe she's talked to Maxim. They seem pretty close."

Alex made the final call. "Hello, Beatrice. Is Mother around? What? Where? Yes, I'm sorry too. It's been a nightmare. Thanks."

Sara didn't like what she was hearing. "Where is she?"

Alex resembled a scarecrow, beaten up and limp and picked clean of his stuffing by a flock of mocking blackbirds. "She left for Fort Lauderdale this morning," he answered, somberly. "She's meeting Maxim down there; some kind of big surprise."

Sara's stomach churned.

"We have to leave right now. Come on," David said, leading the charge.

CHAPTER TWENTY-THREE

Leila was no fool. She knew her life was in jeopardy and her chances of escape were slim. Between the injuries and lack of any significant food and water, she was growing weaker by the second. The only vestige of lingering hope was her faith in Sara. When the men returned for her the next evening, she tried to feign being unconscious, but the agony was insurmountable; she couldn't stop herself from crying out as they picked her emaciated body off the bare cot, grinding jagged bone against raw nerves. They gagged her, but didn't bother to bind her arms or legs; it was clear she was too weak to offer much resistance. The man who earlier suggested raping her tossed Leila over his shoulder like a sack of grain. He carried her through narrow corridors and up a couple of flights of steps, finally emerging on deck.

It was night time, but the stars were hidden by the glow of a nearby city. The lights, even though they were dim, hurt her eyes. Leila resorted to squinting in an effort to see her surroundings. The boat she was being held on appeared to be a commercial vessel. Looking around, she saw hulking cruise ships, cargo barges and tankers docked in the distance. She didn't have any idea where in the world she was. It could be anywhere…anywhere warm, at least.

The men transferred her from the ship that served as her dark prison to a small motorboat. One man navigated while the other sat next to her with his thick, tattooed arm draped across her lap. She wondered if it was to prevent her from jumping overboard. It was a quick trip across the harbor. Despite her dire circumstances, the fresh air was a gift.

As they approached a line of large yachts, Leila thought about Alex and their short yet amazing time together. Tears started to well up in the corners of her eyes. She went to wipe one away but stopped and blinked, straining to see where they were headed. She was shocked when she read the name painted across the back of the stern. *The Unrepentant Siren* was welcoming her back to safety. Her heart leaped at the thought that Alex found her. Maybe this whole harrowing episode was about securing a ransom. *You did it, you saved me. Thank God.*

The small boat motored slowly toward the rear landing of the larger ship. Leila craned her neck to see if Alex was standing onboard like a triumphant hero, anxious to be reunited with his damsel in distress. Instead, she recognized the scowling faces of Luca and Eric. They weren't alone. She shook her head, not wanting to admit the obvious. Alex wasn't there, but someone else was. As the color of the sky began to lighten and dawn began to break through, Leila had the feeling that she was being ushered from one living hell to another.

"Have the accommodations surpassed your expectations, darlin'?" the conniving monster-in-law asked. "Only the best for family."

The gag held back the flurry of hateful expletives Leila tried to scream as her aching body was toted unceremoniously by Eric deep into the *Siren's* bowels. Leila was dumped like refuse onto a single cot in one of the crewmen's quarters. Propped against the opposing wall was a four-by-six oil painting that was badly slashed with a knife.

"Too bad," Eric said as he bolted her in.

Leila was alone again. She ripped the gag from her mouth and screamed in a primal release of fear, rage and hatred. She hobbled over to the door and banged on it with the only hand she could raise. Leila felt as if she had nothing left to lose as she repeatedly cursed her captors. "Let me out, you bastard!" It didn't take long to deplete whatever energy was left in her reserves. She limped back to the single bed and collapsed. Leila was plagued by the same questions over and over: *Why? What did I do?* When she finally emerged from a depressed and despondent haze, she focused on the tattered image starring her in the face. "Charlie," she whispered, the name catching in her throat.

With no point of reference, Leila couldn't be sure if the isolation made time move slower or faster. She didn't know how long she was left to wallow in her solitary misery when someone suddenly opened the lock. She pushed herself into a sitting position and prepared to fight to the death with the last ounce of strength she could muster. She expected the cruel mastermind behind her abduction to sweep in to finish her off, but she was wrong. Luca entered the cramped space. She placed her index finger to her lips, urging Leila to be silent.

"Mrs. Whitfield, I'm here to help you get the hell out of here," she whispered. "Can you walk?"

Leila's heart jumped at her words, "Barely. Maybe with some help." She balanced precariously on one leg as she pulled herself up. "I'm in pretty bad shape; I must have landed on my left side because most everything is cracked and swollen."

"Swing your right arm over my shoulder," her rescuer said, sliding her left one around Leila's waist. "We have to be quiet and quick."

"Why are you doing this?" she asked.

The petite woman struggled to answer under the burden of Leila's weight. "I was hired by Mr. Powers to convince you it would be in your best interest to leave your husband and divorce him. He wanted it done discreetly before anyone could find out who you were, but obviously, he was too late. The kidnapping was underway before I had time to intercede."

Leila didn't understand. "Mr. Powers…Maxim?"

"The Congressman," Luca clarified, guiding her toward the door.

"Alex's father?" she questioned, more to herself than to her rescuer. "I'm so confused."

Luca cracked the door open an inch and peeked out, surveying the passageway. "The two of you crossed paths years ago; things went bad, very bad, and his girl Charlotte ended up dead. He was afraid the family would recognize you and, well…all hell would break loose, or as it turns out, something like this would happen."

Charlie…Charlotte. How?

"Now's our chance; a car is waiting. The Congressman will take it from there."

Leila clung to Luca as she dragged her injured and uncooperative body down the hallway toward freedom. She didn't have time to think about what would happen after she got off the yacht; the immediate risks they were facing were palpable. They were forced to duck into a small storage room when they heard the chatter of people descending the stairs. As the voices faded into the distance, they resumed their trek upward.

As they rounded a corner, Leila heard a shot. The brave woman that was ushering Leila to safety collapsed to her knees and fell forward, landing on her rosy cheek. Blood trickled out of the entry hole in the middle of her forehead. The momentum of Luca's sudden fall sent Leila reeling off balance. She landed with a hard thud against a wall but miraculously didn't go down.

"Where do you think you're going?" the voice behind the gun asked with a familiar, syrupy-sweet accent.

Leila couldn't believe her eyes. Constance stood before her, holding a small revolver in her right hand. It was aimed directly at Leila's pounding heart.

"You?" Leila blurted out.

"Don't test me, Sugar," Constance answered without blinking an eyelash. "I'm a very accurate shot."

~

The sound reminded Sara of her cousins setting off a cherry-bomb on the Fourth of July. The only difference was that it wasn't the middle of summer; it was January, and the sharp crack of thunder came from *The Unrepentant Siren*. Alex and David heard it too and bolted ahead. The trio sprinted around a chauffer-driven sedan with blacked-out privacy windows. They were almost to the gangplank when a voice called, "Alex!" The small group of friends spun around; Ralston was standing next to the car's open rear door, wearing a grim expression.

Sara glanced at David then at Alex. "What do we do?" she asked, conscious of what was at stake. "The boat or your father?"

"He has two seconds," Alex replied, angrily. He trotted back to the former Congressman.

Sara and David watched as father and son exchanged muffled words. The brief meeting culminated in Ralston slipping his son a handgun. Alex slid the steel shaft into the top of his jeans and made a beeline back to the worried couple.

"He said he tried to get her off the boat. He has someone on the inside, but …," Alex started to explain.

"But what?" Sara asked.

David squinted at Alex. "What the hell does that mean?"

Alex shook his head. "He heard the shot. He phoned the police, but no telling how long till they arrive. I can't wait. I only hope we're not too late."

"Sara, I want you to stay here," David said. "It's too

dangerous."

"No friggin' way! Leila's in there," she replied, rushing toward the boat with only her friend's safety in mind. She had charged up the metal plank and through the doors to the main deck before David caught up with her.

He yanked her back by the arm. "Are you insane? You're getting off the boat this instant. This is non-negotiable. Someone is firing a gun."

"I don't give a damn," Sara said angrily.

"Sorry, but I'm not about to risk making Jack an orphan," he replied, sternly. "Go back and wait for the police."

"He's right," Alex stressed. "Leila wouldn't want that."

"We'll find her, I promise," David said.

Sara knew they made sense, but unfortunately, patience was not high on her list of virtues. She was so focused on Leila, she didn't even consider the very real danger they would be facing. Sara felt torn, but she couldn't chance leaving her son without parents. "Fine, I'll go, but be careful. And hurry!"

David kissed her then dashed after Alex, who was already heading down a passage leading to the lower decks.

"God, please help them. Bring everyone back safely," she whispered as she watched the two men disappear into the bowels of the yacht.

Sara was about to open the door to exit, but an overwhelming sensation of fear washed over her. Suddenly, her legs grew surprisingly weak, forcing her to lean against the wall for support. She closed her eyes and took a deep breath, hoping it would quickly pass. Instead, she directly tapped into Leila's calls of distress. Sara listened intently as Leila mentally summoned her, begging her friend to find her before she was killed. *Sara, if you can hear me, that crazy bitch of a mother-in-law is going to shoot me. Please come. I'm in a hallway near the master's quarters on the main deck. Hurry!"*

At that moment, Sara realized the guys had gone the wrong way and there were only seconds to spare. She could sense from Leila's anxiety that Constance was about to pull the trigger. Sara zeroed in on her friend's signal like radar picking up a target. But David's words about Jack made her hesitate and consider the consequences. *I'm sorry, honey, but if I don't do something right now, Leila is going to die.* Determined not to let that happen, Sara somehow found the strength, courage and unquestioning faith to follow the fragile thread Leila's voice created in her mind. As she wandered into the depths of the boat, the increasing intensity of the vibration told her she was on the correct path. She carefully weaved her way through a number of hallways until she heard Constance just around the next corner. The agitated woman was speaking to Leila in a venomous tone.

"Women like you are nothing more than opportunistic parasites. You see a weakness and you latch on without regards to the damage you cause. It doesn't matter one bit that you suck all the goodness and life out of someone. You leave a wake of death and destruction behind."

"What are you talking about?" Leila asked.

"Don't you dare feign innocence! You know exactly what I'm talking about. You didn't care how you seduced and manipulated my dear baby, Charlotte. You drove her to the devil, making her question her values. She was deceived into believing she was someone other than who she was – a good girl, an Ashton. As far as I'm concerned, you killed her. My child's blood is on your sin-stained hands. But what do you care? You were on to the next victim, but not this time, not with my Alex."

"He loves me!" Leila replied defiantly. "How can you do this to him, make him grieve for me and think that I'm dead? What kind of mother are you?"

Constance laughed in a way that made Sara certain that the older woman had completely lost her mind. Sara could tell from their volume that Constance was closer to her than Leila. She knew she had to do something, but what? She had nothing to defend herself with: no gun, no pepper spray, not even a vase to crack over her skull. *I'll jump her from behind. No, that's too risky. She might accidentally shoot Leila…or me.*

"Darlin', I thought you were brighter than that," Constance said, smugly. "You see, you are dead. Only the details need to be finalized."

Oh crap! Sara glanced back down the hall. There was nothing and no one in sight. *Come on, David. Get back upstairs!* Sara had no choice, she started quietly backtracking, hoping to find a door that might open and reveal something, anything, that could be used as a weapon. She turned down one hall and then another, then thankfully spotted a fire extinguisher compartment flush against the wall. Sara pried it open with her fingers and pulled the canister out. She hoped to God it would work.

She stealthily stalked back toward her previous location and listened for the sound of the women's voices.

"Go to hell!" Leila sputtered. Her voice was raspy and more labored. "I'm not giving you my engagement ring or wedding band. You'll have to pry them off my fingers after you murder me, you crazy bitch."

"Have it your way," Constance answered.

Sara couldn't wait any longer. She pulled the pin, stepped around the corner and pointed the hose straight ahead. "Hey!" she yelled, drawing Constance's attention away from Leila. At the same time Sara pressed down on the handle, sending an explosion of white foam directly into the Southern grand dame's face. This caught Constance by surprise, making her stagger backward blindly while reflexively reaching up to protect her eyes. Sara wasted no time. She took two steps forward and swung the heavy metal canister directly at her target's head. It landed with a sickening thud, sending Constance to the ground in a heap.

Leila watched with an open mouth as Sara bent down and grabbed the gun from the unconscious woman's hand. "Thank God you're okay," Sara said, rushing to Leila's side.

"You came, you really came," Leila uttered through stilted sobs. "I knew you would, but I didn't think you would make it in time."

"Of course I did," she replied, hugging her best friend. "But you're probably still in danger. We have to get you out of here."

"Luca," Leila said, hesitating to move. "We have to help her. Constance shot her. She was trying to get me off the boat, to rescue me."

Sara looked down at the motionless woman lying on the floor near them. She could see the bleeding bullet wound in her forehead and knew there was no way anyone could survive that injury. There was nothing they could do now except save themselves.

"We'll send in paramedics after we get off the boat. Let's go." Sara put her arm around Leila's waist and forcefully led her toward the exit. She was worried that loyal crew members, or worse, Maxim, would stop them before they could reach safety. Sara was hopeful when she heard a number of sirens approaching the dock.

"How did you know I was alive or where to find me?" Leila asked as she struggled to keep up with Sara's pace.

"Charlotte...and you," Sara answered, trying to shoulder more of Leila's weight.

Leila shook her head. "It's unbelievable. I can't wrap my brain around the fact that my freshman roommate, Charlie, was Charlotte, Alex's little sister. How could this happen? I still don't understand how it all ties together, and why the hell do they blame me for their lives imploding? I never saw or heard from her again after she left school for winter break. She didn't come back."

"It's a very long and complicated story," Sara answered as they reached the door. She had her hand on the knob when a male voice made her freeze. *Damn it! We're so close!*

"Don't move another inch," Maxim commanded.

Sara turned around and saw he was holding a gun pointed in their direction.

Sara could feel Leila start to shake, but anger suppressed whatever fear she herself had been feeling. She wasn't about to let him harm Leila. "Fuck you, Maxim. Do you hear the police? It's over! We are walking out of here and you're not going to stop us."

Sara turned back toward the door and turned the knob.

"Like hell you are," he answered, angrily. He fired a shot that lodged in the wall a mere inch above their heads.

Before Sara could turn back to face him, she heard a crash. What Maxim didn't realize was that Alex and David had burst into the room from the stairwell the second he fired. They had him tackled and pinned to the ground before he had a chance to react. The momentum sent the revolver flying from his hand; it came to rest in the middle of the polished wood floor.

"You little bastard!" Alex screamed through tears as he wrapped his hands around his brother's neck. "I should strangle you while I have the chance. How could you do this? What sort of sick and vindictive monster have you turned into?"

David pulled Alex off of him. "Stop that, man! We don't need you in prison too. Go to your wife. She needs you."

Alex shook himself free of the restraint and then kicked

his brother squarely in the hip. Leila started crying as they looked at one another. Sara almost joined her as she watched their reunion. Alex ran to Leila and swept her into his arms.

"I'm so sorry," Alex said. "Can you ever forgive me? I didn't know. I never suspected"

"It wasn't you," Leila answered, collapsing against his chest. "And it's over now."

Sara stepped away, trying to give the couple a modicum of privacy. She picked up the gun, the second she had retrieved in the last 5 minutes, and walked over to Maxim, who was still sprawled out on the floor. She pointed the barrel at him. "Max, darlin', you messed with the wrong couple of Northern chicks. I should do the world a favor and blow your brains out."

David stepped closer and pushed her arm toward the ground. "That's enough, Annie Oakley. You don't want the cops coming in here and shooting you by mistake."

Sara looked up at her husband, scowled in protest, but then nodded.

"By the way, I see you listened and left the boat as we agreed," David said. It was clear by his tone that he was not one bit pleased by her change in plans.

Sara shrugged her shoulders. "Sometimes fate intervenes with a more pressing plan."

At that moment, four officers wearing what looked like SWAT gear forcefully pushed open the door with automatic rifles drawn.

"Drop the weapons, now!" one of them yelled. "Arms in the air."

Sara did as she was told and placed both handguns on the ground. It didn't take long for the officers to sort through the critical details surrounding the kidnapping and subsequent violence. They escorted everyone off the yacht. Maxim, along with the crew members who were accessories to the crimes, sported handcuffs. The entire ensemble was unceremoniously stuffed into the back of police cruisers. Leila was immediately taken to the nearest hospital with Alex at her side. Constance, accompanied by an armed policewoman, was taken away in a second ambulance. Not surprisingly, the former congressman was nowhere to be seen.

Sara and David had assured the detectives they would follow them to the station to make statements as part of the investigation. The couple had just climbed into the front seat of the rental car when there was a knock on the passenger side window. Sara nearly jumped out of her skin, but was pleasantly surprised when she turned and recognized the face on the other side of the glass. It was Sean. She opened the door and hopped out to give him a hug.

"Sean, it's so good to see you," Sara said, squeezing him tightly. "Thank you so much for your help today. It made all the difference in the world."

"It's wonderful to see you too," he replied. "I take it you found Leila?"

"We sure did," Sara answered. "She is a badly bruised and probably has a few broken bones, but she is going to recover."

"That's terrific," he said smiling. "I prayed for her. It truly was a miracle that I stumbled across that boat. It must have all been part of the Lord's grand plan."

"I think God must have been working overtime," Sara suggested. Her father's words about some master plan reminded her of Ava's cautionary comments. "Someone recently told me that a powerful force was bringing all sorts of unlikely characters together in the most unbelievable of circumstances in order for the light of truth to burn brightly. I have no doubt you were the final critical piece maneuvered into place so I could solve this mystery before Leila lost her life."

Sean hugged Sara again and kissed her on the head. "My dear child, if you have faith, you possess all the power you will ever need."

EPILOGUE

One year later.

Sara sat at her kitchen table, blowing the steam across a piping-hot mug of cocoa. Chris Isaak soothed her spirit as he sang away in the background. The snow was piling up outside. She looked out the window and watched Jack playing with the dogs. The bad weather kept him home from school and she was glad it did; he would be grown and gone soon enough. Sara didn't take anything for granted anymore and cherished every minute of their time together. Adolescence made him sprout to new heights, leaving him lanky and fairly uncoordinated. She smiled contently as he took aim at the eager canines romping around him in circles. Half the time, the snowballs would hit one of the bigger targets – an unsuspecting Great Dane, while the other half would end up savaged in mid-air by one of the highly enthusiastic and more athletically gifted smaller dogs.

A noise drew her attention away from the comical scene. "You're up," Sara said. "How did you sleep?"

"Barely," Leila replied, yawning. She shuffled over to the chair next to her friend. "You know how it goes."

Sara nodded. "You look exhausted."

"Thanks," Leila mumbled.

"Any news yet?" Sara asked, anxiously.

"Alex should be calling with the results of the plea bargain any time now. Thanks for letting me stay here while he's attending the meeting with the lawyers. It still brings back so many awful memories, I just couldn't stand staying home alone…or worse, going."

"You know you're always welcome here," Sara said. "That's what family is for."

As if on cue, Leila's cell phone rang in her pocket. "It's

him." She flipped it open and spoke into it. "Hi honey, what happened?"

Sara listened silently as her friend nodded several times and carried on her half of the conversation. "I see. How are you holding up?...I'm so sorry. When can I expect you home?...Fine. I'll be there waiting. I love you. Bye."

"Well?" Sara asked.

"Maxim got 15 years with a chance of parole in 11. Constance is getting away with an insanity plea on the grounds that the blow to her head made her unable to stand trial due to severe cognitive impairment. Instead of jail, the evil witch will be spending the rest of her days in a secure psychiatric facility."

"Ouch!" Sara said. "You can't be happy. I didn't realize I hit her hard enough to do permanent damage. I guess I really had some adrenaline pumping."

"Yeah, I would say so. But seriously, Maxim should have gotten life and she should have gotten the electric chair," Leila answered, gazing out at the swirling flakes. "But it's better this way, I guess. It relieves some of the guilt."

"Whose?" Sara asked.

Leila didn't reply immediately, "Everyone's, I suppose."

Sara thought about this answer. It held some validity; pent-up anger, resentment, misplaced blame and a steadfast attachment to old grudges served as lethal poison, infecting good judgment and corroding the core of people's souls. *Although I have to admit, I don't feel one bit guilty about scrambling Constance's brains.*

"I hope Alex can live with the decision," Leila said. "I pray that we can finally put all this behind us."

"You two have so much to look forward to. Plus, what doesn't kill you, and I mean this literally, makes you stronger."

Leila's offered up a weak smile that soon faded into a serious expression. "I can't believe 12 months have passed. How it got twisted into such a convoluted mess, I'll never know. This may sound nuts, but if I could turn back the clock, I would take it back to the day Charlie finished my portrait. If I had responded differently, more sensitively and compassionately, maybe that would have made all the difference for her and the entire family."

"I seriously doubt it," Sara said. "If it wasn't you setting the ball in motion to that family imploding, it would have been someone else. They were incapable of acceptance. Under the circumstances, you were the perfect scapegoat; plus acknowledging their contribution toward Charlotte's death was simply too hard. The portraits were like great big 'wanted' posters, allowing them to focus and concentrate their rage."

"Well clearly, it drove Constance insane," Leila said, flatly. "And Maxim was left behind to pick up the pieces."

"I've thought about this a great deal lately. I've come to believe that Ralston suspected his ex-wife was a few feet short of a yard. He was probably the only one who understood the magnitude of sway she held over Maxim," Sara explained, sadly.

"But he was too late," Leila said. "It's still strange to know that there is a woman out there somewhere in the world who looks so much like me that almost everyone thought we were one and the same. Everyone except you, that is."

Sara smiled. "Good thing for that birthmark."

"And what was Ralston thinking? Like I would have divorced Alex for half a million dollars anyway."

Sara patted her friend's arm. "I never would have thought you would."

"I know," Leila agreed with a smile. "It's been a hell of a rough year. I really didn't think Alex and I could overcome so much. You never know how a tragic event can change you – change your priorities in life. I was one minute away from dying…and yet we were blessed with such a miracle. Faith is something to marvel at."

"Yes, indeed," Sara remarked.

"But really, quite a few amazing things came out of last year," Leila said wearing a sly grin. "I have a surprise for you. I called my dad and set up a time to meet next week."

"What? Oh my, God. I can't believe it. Who are you?"

"I know. It's taken me a while, but Constance forced me to face an ugly side of myself; the part that refused to accept my dad as human."

The muffled sound of a newborn's cry interrupted the conversation.

"Faith is calling," Sara said.

"Yes, she is," Leila replied, beaming. She pulled the baby monitor from her pocket and placed it on the table. "I'll be back."

Tiny mews turned into an impatient wail. Sara watched as Leila scurried up the steps to soothe her fussy little unplanned princess. Shrieks of giggles made her glance back outside. The tables had turned; Jack was lying in the snow, tackled by three Great Danes, an old Springer Spaniel, two Fox Terriers, a fluffy West Highland Terrier and a twenty-something Schipperke. The teenager was paying for his icy assault. Sloppy, wet tongues slathered kisses over his entire face as whip-like, wagging tails served up a thorough beating. Life was good.

Karma, Sara thought to herself. *Sometimes, the planets align and you get exactly what you deserve…and usually what you need.*

9 781563 154386